AF492719

O' Mary Don't You Weep

"The Morner Road Massacre"

Inspired By True Events

Brad DiBello

A Song Of Enlightenment.

Introduction

I had just turned twelve years old when I first became fascinated by tales of green eyed ghouls and beastly bogeymen that live in the closet and lightless space under my bed. When you grow up in the rural country, those stories become amplified by strange sounds in the woods and dark shadowy figures behind trees that are really just tricks of the light. With one eye and ear to the darkness, a vivid imagination can profoundly distort those tales. Still a daring curiosity keeps you from running to a safer place and towards that mysterious strangeness. That is until the day you hear of an even more terrifying and unimaginable true story that if it happened today would run rampant in the news headlines for months. A story that would begin with four aging cemetery stones miles away from my home and lead back to my own front door which stood just a few hundred yards from the site of a crime so brutal and grotesque it is difficult to put into words. This is that story.

Prologue

The Victorian nine room house of my aunt sat on a rise overlooking the Hudson River Valley in the small town of Defreestville, New York three hours north of New York City. Erected in 1860, the gothic gables, peaks and oddly shaped cupola gave it an almost haunting look. As a young imaginative boy, it appeared to be straight out of a classic horror film. The house had been in my mother's family for generations. At one time it was the centerpiece of a working farm with two Dutch style barns also on the property. Typical for the era, the barns were of simple construction. Pine clapboard for siding, an intertwined maze of large wooden beams for framework, a jagged stone foundation, wide oak floorboards to support the massive farm machinery and a steep angled roof to allow for the heavy winter snows to run off. At the triangular peak was a small access door to the loft where tightly bound bales of hay were stored to see the valuable livestock through the long upstate New York winters. Along the length of both sides, a few neatly spaced windows smartly aligned and divided into six hazy man made panes of glass would allow a small amount of light to penetrate the cavernous interior. A light which painted an eerie but poetic scene as beams of brilliant sun peppered with floating dust in the air found their way to the oak planked floor. Adjacent to the property is "The Blooming Grove Rural Cemetery." A small plot of land seven acres in size with headstones dating as far back as 1848. The two properties perfectly divided by a small chain link fence.

As a boy I would attend family picnics at my aunt's house. The older sister of my mother and one of eleven aunts on that side of the family, her rather large home with a grand backyard was the usual meeting place for these reunions. Upon arriving to those gatherings, I would zigzag my way between the numerous Chevys, Fords, Chryslers and other assorted four wheeled shiny metal boxes of all shapes, colors and sizes parked alongside the main house and head towards the crowd in the back. I would be greeted along the way with the welcoming aroma of freshly baked sugary desserts spilling from a half opened kitchen window as I wandered through a menagerie of long folding tables placed end to end which were awaiting the arrival of a steady stream of summer delectables. The day would commence with a few routine hellos shared with a plethora of aunts, uncles, cousins, second cousins and a handful of faces I did not recognize. As my nose grabbed a good whiff of the wavering white smoke from my uncles homemade vegetable soup slowly brewing in the outdoor fireplace, I would sneak away from the backyard where the picnic was taking place to explore the barns and outlying areas of the spacious property. The large main barn, built in 1885, measured forty feet by twenty with massive nine foot wide by twelve foot tall sliding double doors. The doors were so large it would take all of my boyish strength to barely crack one open and disappear from the daylight into the barns darkness. I still remember the stale musty smell inside that was similar to the sudden wall of rankness you break through walking down the stairs of an old damp cinder block basement that most homes in the area were built upon. I stood in wonder as I marveled at the vastness of the interior and the old farm machinery neatly retired in the corners as if it were to say: "I've done my time so now I will rest."

It was during one of these ritual excursions that I decided to jump the small chain link fence that divided my aunt's property from the adjacent cemetery. At the time, chain link fences were low to the ground. This one not more than four feet tall stretching in a straight line along the north border then disappearing to the west down a perfectly graded hill to the front entrance of the gravesite along Route 4, the main roadway through the small town of Defreestville. As a nimble athletic boy, the jump over was quite easy. Brace your arms on the round cross bar supported solidly by an iron rise of perpendicular pipe, swing your legs up and over and off you go. As I rushed across the cemetery property, darting behind a few scattered trees to stay out of view of the elder aunts, uncles and parents who might try to reel me back in like a small fish, I took refuge behind a large square concrete catacomb that stood in the center of the cemetery. With the distinct clanking sound of a heated game of horseshoes my uncles were playing in the distance which seemed to poke holes in the summer air, I would slowly wander through the weathered marble headstones that were scattered throughout the cemetery. If the wind was right, occasionally catching a nose full of freshly dug coffee colored soil from a nearby grave awaiting its new owner. Innocent to the ways of the world, I was just old enough to be blanketed with an ice cold chill and sudden realization these were once living, breathing human beings. Full of hope, ideas, love and dreams like any of us. Call it a first lesson into the realities of life. Being an inquisitive young boy with an insatiable curiosity, it was easy to see why in this entire sea of headstones, four had immediately caught my attention. They were perfectly identical in shape and size standing three feet tall, twelve inches apart and carefully placed in a precise line. The attraction to them proved to be irresistible as all of the other headstones were of random order with no two looking alike. Although I would not remember the inscriptions on the timeworn stones, the imagery of those perfectly aligned oval topped figures protruding from the earth would stay with me to this day, not only for the significance of their presence, but as a reminder to the fragility of human existence and how quickly time disappears until our own mortality comes into question. A question the young family in this story never had a chance to ponder in the horror of their gruesome last minutes.

Not far from my aunt's house, five miles to the southeast in the same town of Defreestville, was my own childhood home. Similar to my aunt's, the house sat on a hill overlooking the Hudson River Valley. It was a simple but sizeable eight room rectangular structure of early 1970's construction. Dressed in white aluminum siding, the house rested on nine acres with large front, back and side yards. The front and back yards met with neighboring homes to the north and south. To the west, the main driveway spilled down a slight grade onto Best Road which led to the small City of Rensselaer.

The side yard to the east was joined by a heavily wooded area which easily consumed half the properties acreage. The wooded area formed a well-defined tree line I knew well. I routinely passed along it each week guiding a clinkering two cylinder riding mower back and forth as it was my family duty to maintain the summer lawns. The ride was usually accompanied by the distinct odor of gasoline fumes relentlessly floating through the air drowning out the rich smell of new mown grass. These fumes the result of gas mistakenly spilled along the red metal fender of the tractor in an eagerness to fill the hungry fuel tank as the weekly Saturday morning chore was eating into a day without school. Having an endless appetite for adventure, the yards and surrounding landscapes of my home were quickly explored and eventually became too small to spark any worthwhile interest. It was on a late Indian summer Saturday that with a bright boldness I daringly decided to investigate the wooded area to the east that screamed out like a large roadside billboard "adventure this way." Those woods seemed like a glorious uninhabited planet filled with leafy full grown oaks, maples, white birch and pines that appeared to extend for miles. Beneath the trees there was practically no undergrowth so it was quite easy to wander through their vertical rise while the crunching noise of dried leaves from the previous fall under my worn out Converse sneakers interrupted the hypnotic silence. A sound greeted by the heavy smell of winter closing in sprinkled with a dash of ripened fall flavors that seemed to stand still in the air. It was during the exploration of these woods that those boyhood stories of monsters became frighteningly real. As real as the strained breath of my cocker spaniel walking beside me with his dull pink tongue flapping in the breeze as he would usually accompany me on my excursions. That afternoon while I made my way deeper into the unknown, it soon became clear there was light a few hundred yards beyond the trees. That light, a series of rolling hills and empty farm fields. Some with the dark russet earth recently turned after an early fall harvest, others left with a handful of dried pale brown corn stalks in scattered well placed lines, nearly stripped clean of most leaves but still standing tall from the previous seasons planting. To the south was a small apple orchard, trees sown neatly in rows, spaced far apart and running along the side of a slight hill. At the base of the orchard, I could see the remnants of what appeared to be an old milk delivery truck. The decaying shell of the truck was overgrown with weeds taller than I was and a rusty crimson color crept through her once bright white metal frame and body as if the earth was saying: "I will reclaim you." Now that I had a better perspective of what lie beyond the woods next to my home, it seemed much easier to continue further on my adventure as the fear of the unknown seemed to dissipate the same way the rows of corn to the east slowly disappeared into a ribbon of fall colors. With an unfulfilled curiosity and my faithful canine companion in tow, I decided to head towards the old decaying milk truck. Sniffing my way between columns of manure saturated air from a nearby horse corral that wafted towards me with a slight slap to the senses. Not expecting to find anything other than the hollow being she had become and too timid to peek inside, my imagination ran rampant as to what hidden treasures could possibly lie within its pyramid of compartments. What an adventurous life that truck must have led traveling the community with its daily deliveries of nourishing solid white goodness used for making butter, cheese, ice cream and of course to top cereal. Naturally, these are the things a boy thinks about on such adventures. The anxious walk took me to the bottom of a small valley one hundred yards or ten minutes from the woods I started out from. The valley cut in two by a tiny meandering stream that this time of year barely had enough energy to move the small amount of stale muddy water it still held on to as it seemed to simply lie in wait for the rains of spring to bring it back to life. As I walked along the bent over yellow wheat grass adjacent to the stream, my attention suddenly turned to the backside of an aged grey barn fifty yards beyond the rotting milk truck. It was a two story behemoth. Rising up from the horizon enough to cast a shadow larger than itself over the picturesque countryside. A few feet past the barn was a narrow stone packed road. A sight of peculiar familiarity. My parents drove my family and I down its winding path to the home of one of our babysitters a few miles away. Growing up with seven rambunctious brothers and sisters, we made that drive often. Those trips, piling eight kids into a small maroon station wagon adorned with fake wood paneling as the faux wood look was all the rage, usually left me pressed against the back right side window of the car. This provided a clear view out of the playfully fingerprinted glass. I would ride in reflective silence as I listened to the banter and exploits of the day exchanged between my parents and siblings, the whole time trying to determine which of five sisters brought the pungent odor of a fruity perfume into the car. On the drives back home from the babysitter, being pinned against the window of the kid packed car, I could easily see the front entrance of that exact same aged grey barn I just stumbled across on my walk. Although I had a sense of what the ghostly interior could have looked and smelled like as it was nearly identical to the barn on my aunt's property, those numerous drive-bys from the sitter often left me wondering what was kept behind the large weathered wooden doors and what secrets the mystical inside might hold. A mystery now answered in the chilling and inconceivable story I'm about to tell you.

My expeditions continued for years around those magnificent fields, old rotting milk truck and the aged grey barn. It was not until years later those childhood tales of green eyed ghouls and beastly bogeymen would become real. That was the day I learned those rolling hills and that majestic property I explored as a young mischievous boy, were the site of the worst crime Rensselaer County, New York had ever seen. A story just as horrifying today as any Hollywood could conjure up using all its gruesome imagination. It's the story of a middle aged dairy farmer found lifeless in the same fields I had roamed in wonder, the finding of a second man shot to death in a neighboring barn, but more so, the terrifying murders of the entire family that lived on that farm. A wealthy and well liked family of three children and a widowed mother that were bloodied, beaten, dismembered with an axe and buried beneath that same barn I would often pass with strange curiosity coming home from the babysitter's. A crime that sparked an investigation for a cold blooded killer or killers that would cover the entire United States and to this day has never been solved but lives on in photographs stored in the Library of Congress. An atrocity that left the small town of Defreestville, New York in shock and horror as police scrambled to determine a motive and locate a suspect. The only tantalizing clue, an eerily confusing hand written note riddle like in nature that simply read: "Italian meat and American made sausage imported from Rome Italy."

The slaughter that occurred in those fields I explored as a young boy is a haunting yarn that stays with me today, wrapped tight in a thick blanket of mystery and astonishing coincidence. Coincidence in that the bodies of that innocent mother and her three children, brutally hacked to death on December 12th, 1911 at 33 Morner Road in the town of Defreestville, only a few hundred yards from my childhood home, are now buried five miles away in "The Blooming Grove Rural Cemetery." The same small cemetery adjacent to my aunt's house where they lie resting restlessly underneath those four perfectly aligned headstones I discovered there as a boy one summer day at a family picnic.

This is the true story of that massacre.

CHAPTER ONE

The Thing About Summer

My name is Edward "Dennis" Donato. People call me Ed. Farmhand by trade. It's Tuesday morning December 12th, 7:35 by the Gilbert clock hangin next to the pantry. I'm sitting at the breakfast table and everyone here is going to die today. Don't know why I ended up doing it. Just one of those things I guess, the other man that lives inside the man. Driven by some kind of madness brought on by mediocrity, that is I mean, when you're broke, all you do is work with nothin to show for it and the answer to your dreams is sittin only three feet across but she still doesn't know you exist. A cold recipe for brewing up this fiery indifference to being a member of this so called human race. A life sentence of the mundane. No telling what a man would do when his conscious is silenced by the thought of this tortured life being a permanent thing, without any kind of real living. Ya know, the kind of living rich folks are doing with their summer houses lit up like Christmas trees, fancy parties every night, garages full of Packards and Peerless touring cars, three trips a year to Europe or some other God damn exotic place. This has become the bane of my existence. Eventually you give no nevermind to damnation forever or the sanctity of life. My own private death sentence.

So what is death anyway? One minute you're here the next you're not. So what if I bring theirs a little sooner, I mean it's gonna happen to all of us anyhow. Like those stinkin corpses of dead animals rotting alongside the road with the life kicked out of them from the front fender of some Henry Ford. While most folks are busy saving up their pennies for the end, time just passes by until it finds them. Death that is. Hell, their eyes are lucky to see sixty or maybe seventy summers and most don't bother counting them anyway. That's the thing about summer, ya never know which is gonna be your last. This is what I told myself about it all, just a little self-convincing to justify what's about to happen. I didn't always feel this way about being above ground. Damn, was only a few years back I was a boy myself with nothing but hope in my pockets but lately, well let's just say I'm not right anymore. I'm breathing and blood is pumping but these days I feel like the walking dead, barely alive in my nothingness. There's some kinda wicked power comes over you when you got nothin to lose still I never gave thought to takin a human life until this morning. Always tried to stay on the right side, maybe strayed a couple times like liftin a few cans of Sniders beans from the grocery when I was hungry but nothin this evil was ever in my mind. I even tried churchin up a few times thinkin I might find an answer. I talked, but no one listened. So here I am at the breakfast table with this family that loves each other and I'm going to end them all. While they talk across and sideways from me, I stare into my darkness looking past each one of them as they exchange their happy little antidotes. God I despise their stories. Guess cause I don't have any of my own, well you know, the happy kind anyway. This mother and her three children together in the kitchen must make quite the postcard image. The cast iron stove blazing away in the corner spewing the smell of fresh biscuits my way from a half cracked window, the speckled blue tin pot of coffee spouting a steady stream of steam into the cold morning and all of them laughing together. It's the sorta picture I've never been part of. Seems like a shame to wipe them all out, but I've decided they have to go.

The farm I live and work on is owned by the Morner family. Dairy, chickens and some feed corn on ninety acres in the town of Defreestville five miles east of Albany, New York. A small farming town with lots of fields, rolling hills and plenty of nothin to do. Folks here like it that way. The property is made up of a twelve room house, large cow barn, smaller hay barn, carriage house, wood shed and a hen house surrounded by divided plots of neatly planted corn, cow pastures and an apple orchard. The barns are one hundred feet from the house which sits back thirty yards off the main road that runs from here to the town of Averill Park. Drivin up here you wouldn't see much other than random dirty white corn silos stickin up outta the ground with silver tops shining in the sun like some kinda Egyptian monument. The cramped kitchen table we're huddled around isn't very large, a simple four legged slab of pine barely four foot by eight with walnut stain worn from years of steady use and six narrow but sturdy wooden chairs. Sittin close to each family member, it's easy to see into their eyes. If they only saw what was in my eyes. At the head of the table is the mother of the family Mary Morner. I always liked her. She inherited the farm from her husband Conrad who died here five years ago. They don't talk much about that or the business of the farm. All I know is they found him in the field. The life had just gone out of him, strange since he was only fifty six. Death found its way here again soon after that. I heard the neighbor, Frederick Kipp, shot himself in his stomach with a Colt revolver while sittin in his barn last year, then while he lie there bleeding out, set the whole thing ablaze. Not exactly the way I'd wanna go. No particular reason was said to why he did it, he just did it. I'm sure that made for some tasty dinner conversation round here. Can't understand why the doomed surround this farm.

Mary and Conrad married when she was twenty two years old. They must of had somethin cause they stayed at it for thirty one summers. She was one of thirteen children. Christ can you imagine that many lives to be in charge of? Her ma and pa had to be beside themselves to put that much food on the table seven days a week. Me, I've no siblings to speak of, hell I have no real friends either. None that I could talk to about girls, places I've been or the picture show I saw last week at the nickelodeon in the City of Troy which is ten miles from here. It was a grand one called L'Inferno about a fella findin some kinda salvation at the top of a mountain. I liked it cause it was made by an Italian and the fella in the movie ends up in heaven after goin through some kind of hell to get there. Kinda my story but after today, don't think I'm gettin in. To heaven that is. Already seen hell in steerage of a five hundred foot steamer coming to America with 2,000 other eager dreamers crammed in the hold like canned tomatoes. The belly of that ship included every horrid odor God put on this earth which was sucked, not by will, up both nostrils with every dreaded breath. Before the trip they gave us a guide explaining what to bring: three Guernsey or flannel shirts, six pairs of stockings, one pair of good stout shoes, one pair of good stout boots, one suit of warm outer clothing, one suit of light clothing, an extra pair of trousers, one light cap and one warm cap or southwester. My entire life packed into a grubby grey canvas bag and flung loosely over my shoulder.

Sitting to Mary's left is Edith, the oldest daughter. Around twenty two. A raven haired brown eyed sturdy farm girl. Aside from farming, her favorite thing was to read the trendy magazines and keep up with the fashion of the day. She wore her hair short in a bob which I didn't like but was all the rage. I'd see it everywhere walking the streets of the other nearby City of Rensselaer when I had free time, which was usually never. Being the oldest daughter, she seemed to follow everything Mary did like she was gonna take over one day. She never bothered me much until last night when she played a cruel joke on me. Looking back, that might have been the thing that set me off but I'll talk about that later. The root of my real madness is sitting across the table. The youngest daughter Blanche. I love her. I loved her the first time I saw her. She's eighteen years old, tall, slender, long sandy blonde hair and bright blue eyes. A German beauty. She's the girl I always dreamed about meeting, for as long as girls mattered anyway. She pays me no attention and that's making me crazy. Tried everything to get her to notice me. Slick my hair back just right with Morgans pomade I get every week at the Rexall, trimmed my sideburns that I usually wore long, shirt tucked in and overalls rolled at the ankles with a perfect fold. Best I can do for being an itinerant farmhand. I greet her with a big ol' smile every time I see her and try to stand next to her when I can hoping she'll notice but still nothing. If she only knew what a grand husband I would make. Never had trouble with getting girls before. They seemed to like my dark skin, brown eyes and black hair. I always dressed nice when I could, my favorite getup being my brown pinstriped suit, my only suit that is. Father and I bought off the sale rack at Steigers department store in Springfield. Pa pitched in for my size eight matching brown wing tip shoes, real dandies. When I was all done up, all the girls noticed. The one thing goin against me is I'm not very tall. Five foot six and one half inches to be exact and one hundred twenty one pounds. Still, there's some kinda fire in me for this girl that's ragin out of control. More than just the usual obsession a young man of twenty three would have for someone like her. She's all I ever think about. My other problem is sitting to Mary's right, Blanche's older brother Arthur. He's suspicious of my infatuation with his sister and the uncontrollable lust that runs wild in my head like that pack of mangy coyotes we see trotting through the east field. He sees it in my eyes from the way I look at her. I'm sure he knows what I'm thinkin. Hasn't said anything of it yet but the looks he gives me are like ice picks, brilliantly cold and disapproving. Arthur was a mature thirty one years old and helped manage the farm with Mary. He was serious and hard working. His older brother Jesse, who ran his own farm just two miles away, was really in charge of both enterprises. Arthur did way more than his fair share of work, ya know, where the younger kid tries to impress his older brother.

Working for the Morners wasn't all bad. Mary was always good to me and the family treated me well, as long as I kept up with my work. The job itself though is hard and the thought of being doomed to this life is burning some kind of evil into my brain to the edge of complete madness. My days are spent fixin things, shoveling up after the animals, helping with the milkin, working in the fields, ya know, typical farm chores that wear you down to nothin every day. If you really want to understand the thing, we'll have to go back four months to how I got into this mess in the first place.

One Turn On The Trail

Earlier in the year on August 10th, I went to the Empire Employment Agency at 1 Howard Street in Albany looking for work. Any work, I was flat broke. Like most of us who came to America with nothing, we took whatever job we could. I arrived here three years ago from Tivoli Italy which is east of Rome. Ma died a few years before that from pneumonia so it was just me and father. Father and I seemed to be more like acquaintances than kin but Ma, we were really close. I was her only child and she made me feel that way. I wonder if she was still around things mighta been different. I loved Italy but the thought of a better life brought Pa and me here to the states. Now that I'm here, seems like it's all just the same thing over again. Wandering from place to place and job to job. No money, no steady girl, no prospects. A few weeks after arriving in New York City, we made our way on the New York Central Railway to the City of Hudson which was one hundred miles north. Although New York was electric with lots to do, I didn't care for the crowds and filth. So many people in so little space. It was nothing like the open air of Tivoli. We're country folks at heart so that's why father and I headed upstate. From Hudson we traveled east and finally settled in Springfield, Massachusetts. The town was full of factories where they made everything from Springfield Rifles to Indian Motorcycles. There was lots of work and lots of trouble in the lawless Main Street saloons and back alley brothels. Pa and I took jobs at the Indian Orchard textile mill on Front Street. Being inside on that assembly line all day around those loud unforgiving machines with their constant clanking back and forth, up and down, weaving their endless parade of cotton just wasn't my thing. Father knew why I had to set off on my own away from city life. He and I weren't very close but I did promise not to go far and write whenever I could. I took the Delaware and Hudson to the City of Troy which was another forty five miles north of Hudson. I found work on a barge that brought garbage up and down the Hudson River. The never ending stench of discarded fruits, vegetables and other inedible remains wasn't my cup of tea either so on the 10th, I wandered into the Empire Agency hoping to improve my lot. With jobs in short supply, they had nothing but said something might come up soon as I was quite capable of performing most types of manual labor. Just as I was leaving, Arthur Morner phoned in explaining that he needed an extra hand on his farm in Defreestville. Knowing it was only a few miles away, the agency suggested I pay him a visit. Man, what dumb luck. If it had been only ten seconds later that Arthur called, I would have been on my way out of there and this entire family would still be alive. As fate would have it, this random meeting would be the beginning of the end for all of us. One turn on the trail.

The next morning, I set off for 33 Morner Road in Defreestville, the address the agency had given me. They informed Arthur I would be arriving at 7 AM. I hitched a ride with a farm equipment salesmen in the back of his old beat up Mercury high wheel truck. A few sputters and puffs of gray smoke aside, we headed east up the hill from Rensselaer, past a big white church that sat on the road that led north to nearby Troy, then off on a short drive through some grassy fields where we bounced along the narrow dirt road to my new job. I felt relaxed driving through what looked like a nice small sleepy town. When I arrived at the Morners, I nodded a quick thanks to the driver and saw Arthur there to greet me at the front door. Was surprised to see someone so young. I had expected him to be much older. Ya know, skin like leather, grey hair and wearing a pair of worn out overalls. A farmer. To my surprise, he was a well-dressed, well-spoken young man. Wasn't expecting him to be wearing brand new denim, a collard wool shirt and matching jacket. Was easy to see he musta had means. After a quick hello, he seemed to want to get right down to the business of it. The agency told him of the places I worked before so he didn't have too many questions other than the usual small talk to get to know me. We walked over to the main barn where he showed me the six spirited horses and one dull eyed bull that were posted there. The barn was well organized and evenly divided into stalls that were dedicated to milking the cows. "You know how to milk don't ya" he asked in a slow but precise voice. "Sure do" I said, even though I had never done it before. Couldn't be that hard, I had seen it done once visiting my cousin back in Italy. He pointed to the fields behind the barn that seemed to go on for miles in three directions, ran his finger in a semicircle along the horizon and braggingly said: "This is all ours." Not far off just below the shadowed tree line, I turned to see a herd of forty or fifty black and white cows heading our way. It was feeding time for them. By the time I turned back around, Arthur had already gone and started filling the feed troughs with the heifers bovine breakfast. It was plain to anyone he had been a farmer his whole life. The task was done in nothin but a few minutes. "Follow me" he said while he walked back to the house: "I want you to meet the family and show you to your quarters." That made me feel real good. It seemed I had the job. The agency must have really talked me up. We entered a side door directly into the kitchen of the spacious and comfortable looking farmhouse. It was easy to see the family did real well farming. The kitchen walls were covered in pale yellow wallpaper with pictures of small brown chickens that repeated themselves up and down. A bright assortment of cast iron pots and pans hung over the double wood stove and a great six foot tall cherry china cabinet sat kitty corner. Through clear glass doors etched with pictures of fruit, I could plainly see it was filled to the brim with fine white china decorated in red patterns of oak trees and acorns, matching soup bowls, an array of drinking glasses and a single drawer in the middle half opened and packed with silver knives, forks and spoons. There was a sitting room to the left that was separated from the other rooms by two large wooden doors with six panes of smoked glass in each. Inside was all done up with a paisley maroon sofa trimmed in hand carved wood round the edges, two identical sittin chairs, the finest flowered cloth wallpaper I had ever seen and a chestnut brown upright piano in the corner. I could see the staircase to upstairs and a washroom just down the short hallway. Was nice to see they had indoor plumbing, most country folks didn't and that awful outhouse gets mighty cold in the winter. Arthur's mother

Mary had her back to us leaning over the wood stove. "Ma" he said, "Here's the new guy Ed." She turned with a half-smile, walked over and shook my hand with a firm but friendly grip: "Glad to have you, the harvest is almost here and we could really use the help." Sitting at the kitchen table was the oldest daughter Edith. She had been watching the whole time and looked over to give me a quick and dismissive nod. "That's my younger sister, she's the one in charge of milking" Arthur explained. Then in a blink, my life would have new meaning. I heard the hollow echo of slow footsteps coming down the oak staircase to the side of the hallway. Still trying to take in the menagerie of domestic sites around me, out of the dark hall walked a vision of the purest light. There she was, Blanche Morner. As we both turned to look, Arthur spoke in a flip second hand voice: "Oh, and that's my little sister, this is Ed the new hand." With a full smile, she walked right past me. Left in some kinda trance, I didn't hear a word of her soft sunlit greeting: "Hello, nice to meet you." My eyes followed along as she found her seat at the table. She was wearing a long blue cotton dress running almost to the floor. The deep navy color broken up by a pattern of repeating white lilies topped off with a one inch wide lace collar neatly buttoned round her neck. Her faded brown leather shoes musta had a two inch heel giving her five foot eight inch frame the height of some kinda Greek goddess. She looked, talked and smelled like a dream. I was smitten. Love at first sight. I forgot about why I was even here. The first time you see a site like her you'll just never forget it. Mary offered me some breakfast and I took a seat at the far end of the table. Been awhile since I had a good meal and man, one thing about farmers is they sure do know how to eat. What a spread. Thick juicy bacon, fried eggs, stewed potatoes, fresh squeezed orange juice and a bottomless basket of golden brown homemade biscuits. Didn't want to seem too greedy, but since they had so much, just kept eating until I had my fill. I listened closely while the family traded stories about the latest news sprinkled with a little country gossip. Seems a guy named Calbraith had just flown his airplane clear across the United States, something that meant nothing to me but was still interesting to hear. Would have stayed there all morning but knew there was a day's full of chores to be done. Arthur and I left the girls to the cleaning up and we got on with it. He took me upstairs to a large bedroom directly over the kitchen. "This is yours" he explained. Seemed a nice space. Pretty simple. A single bed pushed up against the side window which gave me a clear view of the barns, a small work desk with a single drawer in the center and a four foot by two foot closet with some ragged work overalls and a worn out cotton shirt sharing a single thin wire hanger. Arthur went on to say, "You're welcome to these, they were left by the guy before you". He then pointed down the hall to the rest of the bedrooms. "Those are ours, no need for you to be down there, so let's get to it."

So it was, I came to live and work on the Morner farm. The family seemed agreeable and I clung to the thought of better days ahead. Little did I know, the next few weeks would become nothing more than a slow death for me.

The Day Before You Came

The thing about Blanche Morner is she doesn't know how perfect she is. A beautiful, simple-minded, warm-hearted country girl. She went to the Blooming Grove Reformed Church every Sunday and just last week, her and Edith joined the Christian Endeavor group to help more needy folks in the area. I remember myself goin to church a few times. Thought it might do me some good, I thought it anyway. Blanche had a head full of dreams and had planned on becoming a horse doctor. She really loved her carefree life. Learning to cook from her mother, her weekly piano lesson and of course visits from her best friend Vera Vanderberg. The two would stay up late on Friday's talking way into the night even though there were always chores to do first thing. Vera was from Troy and although the Morners lived in the country, they were still not far from there and the towns of Averill Park and Snyder's Lake. Both only about five miles to the east. The family didn't visit the nearby towns or cities much and were happy being at home. Sometimes for a special occasion, they would have me ready the carriage for a ride to the Crooked Lake House in Averill Park for dinner. I stayed home to my miserable meal of pork and beans. On the last visit from Vera they mostly talked about how much they missed summer now that winter was almost here. Winters are rough in upstate, lots of bitter cold and snow sometimes clear up to the windows but summers in the country are peaceful and the livin is easy. The stars in the sky on sparkling August nights were like a billion blue points of never ending light. Songs of the crickets took over from the warblers just after sundown and would occasionally be interrupted by the croaking bull frogs down by the pond. Of course there was always the thick foulness of the animals in the barn which we all got used to, eventually, you come to kinda miss that smell. On moon-drenched nights under brilliant white light, I would sometimes see Blanche all alone walking the apple orchard that sat on a rise behind the main barn. The orchard was so close to the tall grassy fields filled with glittery green flashes from hundreds of fireflies, the night would light up all around her. God she was beautiful. She stayed in my fevered mind all day and night.

It would not be until early fall when the leaves were a mix of red and gold that I finally got up the courage to ask her on a walk. We were in the barn finishing up milkin for the day when I asked if she wanted to come along on a small chore Arthur had given me. Seemed there was some bad fence in the north pasture. "Hey, gotta get to some fence fixin, the leaves are turned and it might be a nice walk, wanna come?" Seemed like a whole three minutes to get those words out. She stopped for a second, looked towards the colorless light in the milky window and replied, "OK I guess." Not sure if she agreed because she wanted to go with me or was just fillin in the day between chores. When the word "OK" from a girl like her falls on anxious ears, there's an excitement that vibrates every nerve. My breathing and heart raced. Maybe there was a chance with her.

We set out through the north pasture for a corner of the farm twenty minutes away. She walked tall and confident through the stubborn weeds and wore a slight timid smile on her face, me on the other hand had my head half down while a million thoughts skated through it trying to think of how to get some kinda conversation goin. Not like me to not have anything to say to a girl but she left my tongue in a knot. We walked without a word for five minutes until I finally asked about her plans to become a veterinarian. "Hey, I hear you're learnin about tendin to animals?" Her smile went from slight to sizeable. She started on about her love for horses and how she liked the science of taking care of them using words like anatomy and gastronomy. Once she started talking it was obvious she was in love with the idea of becoming a horse doctor. She went on for ten minutes and even if I had something to say, couldn't have fitted it in. After sharing her ambition, she looked over at me with a sympathetic understanding on her face and we fell back into an awkward silence. Her smile began to shrink. I could plainly see she thought her words were well above my education and vocabulary. I felt beneath her. *Even worse* she thought I was too. My intoxicating dream that she and I would become a thing was quickly turning to black and nothing but dashed hopes were left. When we got to the damaged fence, she suddenly turned and said, "I best be getting back, see you at supper." My dream was left splintered like the broken fence post. The next few days, Blanche seemed to do her best not to stand too close to me or talk about anything besides work. It felt like being put on some medieval rack to die a slow tortured death.

Deaths Door

When you're an eighteen year old girl, boys, being silly with your friends and gossip are what matter most. Death is the furthest thing from your mind. Eventually you see it first-hand like when Blanche's father died a few years ago but it surely didn't make sense to her that one day he was just gone. She missed her dad and from what I heard he was always good to all of them. He never raised a hand and worked hard every day, sometimes well into the night to take care of them. Although her life was simple, I know there's not much else she wanted.

Our days on the farm went on with the usual repetition until the boredom was shattered one evening by a recent visit from Vera. The two girls talked in the parlor while I sat unknown to them in the kitchen. Before long, the conversation turned to me working here. The parlor doors were left slightly open so I heard every word of Blanche explaining to Vera how she knew nothin of me other than my name was Ed and I came from Italy. She was sure her ma and brother knew all about me because they hired me from the agency. I can still hear that sweet angelic voice as she spoke: "He started with us in August and seemed real polite at first. I even thought he was kinda handsome. You know, like the pictures in the magazines of the boys with sun tans and wavy black hair. I could tell by the way he looked at me sometimes that he liked me. He didn't say much but he did talk about Italy a lot with my brother. While we're milking, there isn't much else to do but fill the barn with chin music." Hearing her say she thought I was kinda handsome got my heart racin, that excitement didn't see three tics of the second hand when the conversation took a nasty turn along with my mood. "I guess it all got weird a couple weeks ago" she went on in a dark brown voice. "I would always see him staring at me, not in a good way where someone smiles and makes you feel welcome, but more of a blank slate, like he was looking past me at something else. Sometimes I would even see him outside at night pacing back and forth looking up at my bedroom window. At first I thought it was sweet but then, well it got kinda weird. He started putting his hand on the back of mine when we would first say hello to each other in the barn every morning before milking. Didn't think much of it at first and found it kinda cute that a boy might actually like me. Since he seemed so polite, I didn't think I needed to say anything to Mom or Brother about him touching my hand, besides, he was still almost a teenager himself and not much older than me, anyway, I just thought it natural for him. Everything took a turn last Wednesday. After our usual 'good morning' to each other, his light touch on my hand turned into a firm grasp of my upper arm. He looked in my eyes and it was like he was asking me for something but without asking. It startled me because he grabbed me so hard and I wasn't expecting it but he just stood quiet and didn't do anything. Don't know if it was harmless or not but I kept it to myself, anyway, that's what I know of him."

A week later on Monday December 11th was the night I became a monster. After supper, I sat in the parlor across from Edith while Blanche slowly picked out the notes to "Amazing Grace" on the brand new Homer upright piano the family had purchased with some of the money their father had left them. Watching her play, I could no longer restrain this out of control wildfire for her that's raging inside. I started thinkin bout the right words to tell her how I felt. I played my speech over and over in my head so I could get it just right when my thoughts were suddenly interrupted by the sound of the two girls giggling. It was that girly sound teenagers make when they're gossiping about a classmate or up to some kinda prank. A half laugh they were trying to hold in. Guess the joke was on me when I felt the slight crunch of paper stuck to my back as I sunk deeper into the paisley sofa. Unknown to me, Edith had pinned a loosely torn note to my shirt that read: "Italian meat and American made sausage imported from Rome Italy." Because I wasn't the sharpest tool and just a greasy I-talian to her, Edith took every chance to jab at me. Since they were both laughing, Blanche must have been in on the farce too. That's even worse than her indifference to me and more salt for the fresh wound. The note was poking fun at the Italian sausage links I bought on every trip I made to Rensselaer but I'm sure it had some kinda deeper meaning to them. The corner deli on 3rd street there was run by a family of immigrants from Sicily. I loved that place. The smell of hanging cured meats, squeaking of the crooked floorboards when you walked through the narrow aisles and the site of the large banded pickle barrel at the checkout counter spilling a sour taste into the air all reminded me of being back home in Tivoli. I wrote my father in Springfield just last week explaining how much I missed Italy and wanted to go back. Maybe join the army or somethin and go fight the Africans. I hadn't been able to mail the letter yet and it sat on the desk in my room. Quickly realizing this was not the time to speak of my love for Blanche, I stood up without a sound and tried to hide the embarrassment on my face. That was the when I felt my mind go to a place it had never been. Suddenly all the years of torment and misery in my life seemed to be bubbling to the top like a boiling pot of water waiting to see the spaghetti tossed in. Without a word I slapped the note down on the piano which made a good whackin sound, pulled the coldest look I could muster, aimed it at both of them and made the short but seemingly endless walk back upstairs to my room. Tortured by the missed opportunity to confess my love for Blanche, I sunk to the floor in front of the small closet next to my bed staring at everything I owned and examined my miserable situation. The closet of course was empty. Being a farmhand means little money and a lot of hard work. Long days of drudgery leave you wanting something greater, me, I just want some time to have a little fun and look around once in a while. Sometimes though, I think having more ain't always tops. I know Mary spends all her time running the farm and although she makes good money, she's always troubled over the next seasons harvest or the condition of the fifty or so Jersey cows roaming the fields. The responsibility on her shoulders is considerable so I wonder does she even feel alive? I guess folks might all be better off if they asked themselves, "Why are we saving up for the end without looking around once in a while?" Damn it all goes by fast. What comes after this, hell, I don't know, all I know is maybe there is no difference between a starving dog or fat cat and the only thing that really matters is how much love ya have around you before your number gets called. That's the only thing you'll take with ya. From now on, I'll try to soak up whatever that number is tied to how many summers I have left. Ya know, live more, laugh a little more, tell pa I miss him. All I do know for sure is by this time tomorrow I will have done it. Taken each of their lives.

Later that night, I could hear Blanche talking to Arthur about the look I gave her and Edith in the parlor earlier. The walls of the farmhouse were as thin as a few sheets of note paper so I often heard the muddled talk going on between the family. Arthur, who was still a young man, only thirty one, shared Mary's stress in running the farm. Since Conrad died, the girls always said, "He was a little different, he suddenly became more serious, anyway, he smiles a lot less." Their conversation brought me considerable worry. I knew Arthur had a short temper and I couldn't bear losing my job. It's all I have. As their voices broke through the wall, all that stood out to me like the corn silos around here risin from the earth was the word "creepy" as Blanche described me to Arthur. While she went on about her distaste for me, it felt like a double edged sword piercing the center of my heart. What a slow pain. Her loathsome words rattled around in my brain reminding me of the pool of desire and despair I've been drowning in. Spicy seasoning to a savory nightmare. Like a gasoline bomb, all of my thoughts, hopes and dreams exploded into a million tiny pieces. The wreckage would leave me a madman. I guess that settles it, no chance at any meaningful relationship with her. My love for all things hardened and a hole opened up in my heart where dreams used to be. In that moment of separation between sanity and lunacy, something inside me flipped. Don't know if the demon was always there but he is now. I sat in my silent well of sorrow thinkin the madness might disappear but instead, ideas kept comin. Not the kind of ideas you would speak out loud. One after another like the herd of Jerseys returning from the field. Vile ideas of revenge and retribution brought on by frustration and jealousy for what they had and I didn't began to take shape. So I got on with it. The plan of how to do it. How does one go about killing an entire family without being noticed, then getting the hell away from here after it's done? By sunrise that morning, I had it all figured. Whether Blanche liked it or not, I would finally have her.

The Tipping Point

Tuesday December 12th. After breakfast, I went to the barn. I knew Blanche came to milk around ten so I wanted everything ready for her. She always arrived first while the others went about their chores on the rest of the farm. Blanche never minded milking that much. She daydreamed a lot and was never alone surrounded by all of those mooing and cud chewing cows. I often heard her talking out loud to them like they were all in high society gossiping and having tea in the park. "Did you hear about old Mrs. Astor? What an affair that wedding of her daughters must have been." She spoke to the heifers like they were best friends. Guess it was just to help pass the time but hearing that sweet voice each morning seemed to only add kindling to my fire.

The main barn here is a behemoth. Tools, sickles, blades of all kind hangin from the rafters, shovels, a few dozen large metal milk jugs and an assortment of bridals, saddles and straps for the animals. On a windy day in summer when the doors were left open, that stuff would rattle around clinking and clankin like a store full of Swiss music boxes playing at once. As Blanche arrived, squeezing her long thin frame between the sliding barn doors that were opened just enough to allow a body to pass through, I turned to see just her slender silhouette. My heart began beating faster with anticipation and fear for what I was about to do. The barn was nearly fifty feet from end to end so the long walk over to her from the center seemed like miles. "Hello," that was all I could muster. To her surprise, I quickly reached out and firmly snatched her upper arm. She didn't move. We just stared at each other. Blanche was a strong-minded German farm girl that was not rattled easily but I could feel her begin to shake. We stood in silence for ten or fifteen seconds. Suddenly, to my angry disbelief and without a sound, Arthur entered the barn. He must have stopped in from the fields to get something. I could see both relief and fear still festering in Blanche's blue eyes. I know she was glad to see him but also knew she was troubled over her brother's quick temper. There was no telling what he might do. Before I could blink, Arthur made his way halfway across the barn to us. Without a word and with one motion neither of us saw, he knocked my arm away from Blanche. I was holding her so tight that the force was strong enough to rip away a small piece of her dress before I was able to let go. "What the God damn do you think you're doing" he shouted. I just froze with a blazing stare on my face, like the look the deer give us when we stumble on them in the fields. Arthur continued to yell in a wailing high pitched voice: "Keep your greasy hands off my sister. If you ever touch her or even look at her again, they'll send you back to Italy in a custom pine box." Still half frozen I paused for what seemed like a quarter hour though I know it was only three or four seconds. They both saw the strangest small smile come over my face. Kinda crooked and out of the side of my mouth. My eyes shifted to the right for a second then turned the darkest color of serious you can imagine as I looked directly at Arthur. If fire could have come outta my eyes, I would have lit him up. I spoke just two words as I venomously nodded my head up and down: "I'm sorry." They paused for a few seconds, furrowed their brows and tilted their heads slightly to the left like a confused puppy while they tried to connect the look on my face with the words coming out of my mouth. They realized there were two ways to take my unenthusiastic apology. Was it aimed at Arthur or was it sorry for something about to happen? I took two steps back almost tripping over a milking bucket, caught my balance and went back to work like nothin happened. Each morning we had our own chores to do. Blanche and Edith would do the milking and Arthur the filtering & filling of the beat up steel milk jugs for the trip each night to the milk dealer Horatio Mould. I would feed the livestock and begin to mend what needed mending. I hated the God damn disheartening job but once heard Mary tell the others she was glad to have me. "He's industrious, hard-working and knows tools really well so he's able to fix things around the farm and do all of the other chores that needed to be done." After hearing that, I felt good about myself for once, even if it only lasted a minute. As I went about my tireless work, I looked over my shoulder and caught a quick glimpse of Arthur's face while it slowly turned back to the alabaster white it usually is from the plum red color it had turned after seeing me with Blanche. Even though she was his sister, he sounded fatherly when he put his hand on her shoulder and said: "Listen Sis, if he lays another finger on you, you come tell me, run don't walk, and come tell me." She half smiled, gave him a quick hug and ran off to help her mother finish gathering the fresh eggs from the chicken coop. Then it happened. That moment of no turning back. When the brain simply takes over and says you are no longer human, you are no longer functioning as a sane member of the human race, the tipping point. In a slow zombie like walk, I headed towards Arthur who by this time had gone back to his task of attending to the bridal on one of the horses in the last stall. I noticed a bale stick leaning against the entrance. In a ghoulish trance, I snatched up the four foot long thin wooden shaft and without hesitation or expression on my face, slowly and quietly continued towards Arthur. I looked like one of those walkin Egyptian mummies I saw once at the picture show in Springfield. By now I was well past the stage of reason. With the bale stick in my left hand and images of Blanche haggard and haunted in my head, I slowly reached with my right hand for the five inch bowie knife kept in a worn out brown leather holster at my side. As a farmhand, a dagger like this is common so the family would not have given thought to me carrying it. The walk across the timeworn oak floor to Arthur could not have taken more than ten seconds. He was now slightly bent over examining the lower quarter of the horse. I'm sure he had no idea his time on earth was about to cease. Strangely I had no hesitation and no thought of repercussion, just pent up hatred for all things life had dealt me. And that was it. I drew back the bale stick and with one swift blow stunned Arthur striking him across the middle of his body then again across the side of his bewildered face. Horrified and confused, he quickly turned to see the last image he would ever view on this earth, the look of his killer. Before Arthur could begin to process the sting he felt from the bale stick, in one fluid motion I brought the blade of my now unholstered knife straight across his exposed throat. In less than a second it was done. Arthur, still trying to understand what was happening, had no more than a few seconds of life left in him. Both hands immediately grasped his now opened throat. He dropped to his knees for not more than a second before falling on his side motionless while crimson red blood spilled from between the fingers clutched hopelessly around his neck. His legs twitched one last time and then a tranquil stillness set in. That was that. I began to slowly decipher the event that just occurred. I had never taken a human life. Had seen it done in the pictures but had never given thought to how quickly it could all be over. It puzzled me how difficult it is to build a life but how easy it is to take one. I stared at the body for an entire minute before a bit of reason began to slowly creep back into my fevered brain, erasing what seemed like nothing more than a bad dream. At this point there was no turning back. The madman inside had been unleashed. I was no longer part of the sane world. I sat silent and head down on an overturned milk bucket thinking how my life had just changed forever at my own hands. Without a stitch of remorse running through my blue veins, I immediately began to analyze the possibilities of what would happen next. Will the rest of the family find me? How do I hide this? Should I just run? There's blood on my trousers. The graveness of ending a living, breathing human never entered my mind. After a slow two minutes of cipherin, in some hypnotic cloudburst, I quickly realized that Blanche would be the first to discover my atrocity. She would be back from the chicken coop soon. That would give me little time to hide my deed and no time to have any feelings about it. In a split second of soberness, I knew dragging the lifeless body of Arthur across the floor of the barn would leave nothing but a bloody road map to my crime. I quickly calculated that the fastest way to a clean exit, would be to bury his corpse right in front of the stall where he lies motionless. That's where the floorboards were most accessible. Being a working farm, the barn was littered with tools of all shapes and sizes, ya know for choppin, pulling, cutting, hammering and the like so I knew I could perform this grotesque maneuver with ease. Since my boot was ten inches, I figured each floorboard was twelve inches wide and ten feet long. I figured again that by removing just two of them, the body could quickly be hidden underneath. I got to removing the long iron nails holding the wooden planks in line and with the back end of a hatchet that was hangin on the post next to me, flipped the boards over and dug a few inches into the packed stony soil under the barn. I pulled Arthur by the ankles face down towards the narrow trench and with the bottom of my right foot, rolled his body into the make shift tomb, packed the dirt back in its place, then carefully replaced each board and each nail. I gathered up two armfuls of straw from the stall and covered the dirty puddle of blood that was left behind leaving no sign of the horror that just occurred. In the thirty minutes it took to ready what I figured would be the final resting place of Arthur Morner, the reality of not going unnoticed began to swim through my head like that school of tadpoles in the big stream that fed the watering pond. I knew it was a tough chance if at all I could elude the repercussions of my deed. I couldn't refuse to accept the situation and right there decided the fate of three living, breathing human beings. The others must go too. Desire, anger, fear, hopelessness and voices of my newly discovered demons started to brew together in my head like a slow cooking gumbo. All I ever wanted was that girl to love me, now this madman I've become is going to end her and the rest. A half hour later, Blanche walked back to the barn from the house where she went to leave the eggs she gathered and mend her torn dress from earlier. She saw the neighbor Mrs. Ostrander on the white picket porch directly across the street. Blanche nodded in her typical farm girl way and the two exchanged smiles. The Ostranders were always good neighbors. Chester Ostrander was of some relation to Mary and both families helped each other out when there was a call for it. They too had a well maintained farm and were quite prosperous. As she approached the front doors to the barn, Blanche noticed the strainer on a milk jug to the right. "Guess Arthur is getting ready for the milkin" she thought to herself. The doors to the barn were usually kept open only a foot or two in the winter, that was to keep some of the cold away from the animals. She slipped between the opening, took three hushed steps into the barn and called for her brother: "Art, you there?" There was no reply. The day was cloudy so there wasn't much light comin through the grubby windows. It was normal not to see him when she first entered because he would usually be in one of the stalls attending the animals. She called again - no answer. I could plainly see she was cautious about walking further into the barn. About half way down the center aisle, she called again, still no reply. I heard her say to herself out loud in a whispered voice: "Well, maybe he had to go out into the fields for something." She quickly turned to go back to the house. By now, I had made my way to her from behind one of the big oak beams holdin the place up and was right in front of her. Not more than two feet away. "Ed?" she asked, half curious and half scared. The barn doors were to my back allowing only a small vertical column of fresh light through, not enough for her to clearly see my face, just a black shadowy figure. Half frozen, only her eyes moved as they looked down at my left hand. I was tightly squeezing the bale stick I had introduced to Arthur. In a slightly quivering voice she asked, "Where's my brother?" I returned to the half-smile and shifty-eyed look I gave the both of them earlier and coldly said: "He's not here anymore." She replied, "Anymore? What do you mean?" I looked her in the eye and repeated: "He's not here." I watched all of the strength suddenly leave her body while my knuckles turned white from squeezing the bale stick even harder. She knew something was really wrong. Before she could finish her sentence "wait until I tell my...," I dropped the bale stick, charged forward and was on her. We both fell hard to the ground with me on top. I pinned her by the wrists to the cold winter floor. Even though she was bigger than I was, some kind of super strength came over me. Nothing about her could move, not a muscle, not even a finger. I straddled her with my knees planted firmly on both sides of her slim body but didn't say a word, just stared at her. She knew what I wanted but didn't know if she could stop me. Blanche had two thoughts: "If I fight back he might get madder, he could go over the top and hurt me. If I don't fight back, well then I'm a failure." Blanche was still young while her father was alive but one thing she remembered him sayin was: "You only fail if you stop trying." I could feel her summonsing all the strength her five foot eight inch frame could muster as she arched her back and threw me off. I didn't weigh that much so it was easier than she thought. Blanche jumped to her feet, turned and tried to run for the door. Before she took a single step I reached out and wrapped my hand around her ankle. When she leaned forward to run, she lost her balance and hit the ground hard. Without saying a word, I climbed back on top of her, grabbed both of her arms and pinned her back down by the wrists. The fall must have knocked the wind out of her or she was just so petrified that when she opened her mouth to scream, nothing came out. I could see her struggle to scream again – still nothing. Our eyes locked onto each other. In the queer silence with only the sound of a few random bellows from the curious cows in the background, we tried to read each other's thoughts. She twitched a few times to test my strength before finally getting four words out in a quiet, broken and terrified voice: "It-will-never-happen." Knowing she had a lot of fight in her, I took this to be true makin me even more angry. I reached behind and grabbed the bale stick I had dropped. The next thing Blanche saw was the thin shape of the four foot shaft coming into focus and heading directly at her. With a sadistic swiftness she knew it was coming hard and she knew it was coming fast. The blow connected with the left side of her head and dazed her. She mumbled a little and slowly rolled her head from side to side. The love I had for her had disappeared; only the bloodthirsty beast in me was left. Then, on that dark December afternoon, in that dark dingy barn, on that rough oak planked floor, I reached down, pulled her dress up to her waist and I took her, along with her virtue. For the next minute afterwards, I lied transfixed on top of her in the silence of the cruel afternoon. I could still feel her body moving while she drifted in and out of consciousness. I just knew there was no way back from this. Frozen in fear and madness, I stared at her pretending we were complete strangers hoping that would help me muster the courage needed for what was next. I couldn't let her leave here. I pulled my knife, still bloodied from the earlier dispatch of Arthur, drew back the blade, took one last look into her glassy eyes and plunged it death deep into her left side. The next second was eighteen year old Blanche Morner's last breath. I came to America looking for a future and well, here I am bringing death to this land of possibility. I rose to my knees and paused with a long look of shame that was soon overtaken by indifference. I lied back down on my back beside her while her soul dripped out of the knife wound. This was the second life I had taken this morning. The only thought I had was of the random soldiers I met when I was traveling to the states. They all said that after the first kill, it gets easier. For me it was the opposite, guess the difference is I didn't kill, I murdered. My focus then turned to coming up with a bigger plan. There were still two more living witnesses. I know Mary rarely came to the barn cause the others did the milkin so my thoughts turned to Edith. Since the Ostranders lived so close, just across the street, I knew I had to take the others quick and quiet. I took one last look at Blanche. My love, the only thing I had ever wanted outta this miserable God damn life and she was gone forever by my own hands. There was no time for honoring her or for anything else. I needed to get away from here. I couldn't stand one more look at what I had done so with my head turned and eyes closed tight, grabbed her by the ankles dragging her extinguished body into one of the nearby stalls. I gathered some handfuls of straw to cover her still warm remains and the pool of blood left behind. I picked up the hatchet I used earlier to remove the floorboards along with the now bloodied bale stick and walked to the entrance of the barn. I waited inside knowing the darkness would be to my advantage in surprising my next victim. Mary was still in the kitchen and Edith was not far off by the woodshed collecting timber for the kitchen stove. I called to her in a ghoulish downward lilting voice. My words "Edith, E-d-i-t-h" rode the breeze right to her. She looked in all directions trying to gather where the sound was coming from then looked towards the barn. Without showing myself, I reached between the open doors with just my right arm and waved my hand back and forth calling her over. Curiously she walked towards me. Knowing the neighbors were only yards away, I dropped the hatchet and bale stick and picked up a milkin stool. I thought if I took her down with the blade, there would be no sound but a lot of mess for someone to see. I stuck my head outside of the barn to be sure no one was watching. Edith walked right up to the front doors and *bang*, she met the stool right across the side of her head. Stupefied and dizzy she looked right at me. Seemed she was trying to work out in her mind what the hell was goin on. She swayed slightly back and forth but didn't fall to the ground. I grabbed her and pulled her inside, half walking, half dragging, towards the stall where Blanche lie breathless. This is when I knew I had become an animal. Twenty three years of torment was about to rain down on this poor unsuspecting girl. I threw her to the ground, picked up the bale stick and began driving the pointed end into her still living body. The last blow poked right into the side of her pale head. Moaning and grunting, she raised her arms in front of her face to try and drive off the evil that was standing above her.

My rage began to get worse. Knowing I had to finish the job, I picked up the hatchet with more anger than I've ever known and hammered her with the business end. With her arms still raised in an 'x' in front of her face, she tried to fend off the merciless beating leaving her right forearm clearly broken. I was surprised how strong willed she was. Maybe she was in shock or just confused but she didn't speak a word or utter a sound. The next blow with the hatchet would be the end of Edith Morner. I had struck her with such rage that it nearly took her head off. Way past dead, I continued to pummel her harder until the torn flesh on her face became unrecognizable. My rampage went on, striking her limp body faster and faster. My angered voice grunting with each thud of the hatchet against her mutilated form. I didn't stop until her insides began spilling over. God what have I become? What is this ghastly sickness that brought me to dismiss these people? Still in some kinda primal fury and with three expired bodies in front of me, I remembered there's one more to dispatch. Mary might be the most difficult. She had a lifetime of experience and would not fall easily. I decided to work on hiding Blanche and Edith and let Mary arrive to this barn of death in her own time. Knowing how long it took to dig up the floor where Arthur had been shoved into his make shift grave, I needed to act faster. Behind the row of stalls against the outer walls of the barn, ran a thirty foot trench four feet wide and three feet deep. This is where the crap from the cows was shoveled into each day to keep the stalls from turning into a mangy mud heap. I knew the boards covering the stinking gutter were just loosely thrown on top cause I had cleaned "the pit" so many times before. I tossed aside three of the oak slabs. They were the same size as the floorboards I had removed while burying Arthur only these were not nailed down. The stench of days old refuge coming from the stinkin hole hit me in the face and seemed to cause more inconvenience than taking these three souls. Blanche would go in first. Seeing her one last time, I wish I could've cried but I didn't know how. I dragged her alongside the pit and rolled her in like some school kids rag doll. I picked up Edith with her arms still frozen in front of her face, one broke and one solid but still dead as Abraham Lincoln. The blows with the bale stick and hatchet ripped her clothes and body to pieces leaving her nearly naked. With a light toss, I let her fall on top of Blanche. In five minutes it was all done. I left the pit open knowing there would be a third coming to this death party. Still wonderin if I had been detected or not, I stood in ominous silence while I tried to figure how to lure the last one to her end. I sat down and leaned my back against the stanchion that kept the horses fenced in. With nothing stirring on the usually busy farm and the middle of the day as quiet as midnight, I knew it was only a matter of time before Mary became curious. Waiting for her to investigate gave me time to plan my exit from this horror show. That would be a quick bit of ciphering. I knew the only way out was to get back home to Italy. I figured I could hop the train in Troy, make my way back to Springfield to see pa, then grab a steamer in New York City or maybe Boston. On the other hand, maybe a quick trip to Hudson where father and I lived when we first got to the states and I still had a few not so law abiding friends there to help with my breakin loose of this. Before I came up with an answer, I saw a shadow walk in the front doors. Being in this dark place for so long, my eyes were well adjusted and I could easily see it was Mary. I thought best thing to do was play possum. Let her come to me. In a loud strong voice she cried out: "Ed is that you?" then again, "Ed?" She continued her death walk towards me. In a curiously angry voice she asked: "Where is everyone? We got milking to do." Those were the last words Mary Morner ever spoke. I jumped to my feet. Behind my back was my new weapon of choice, the already bloody hatchet. She stared expressionless and fixated on the blade. Tears formed in her eyes. With a killers smile I spitefully whispered Mary don't you weep. I went to work. One, two, then a third rhythmic blow to the left side of her head and she dropped. Without a cry or quiver I ended her. I continued to beat her even though she was clearly extinguished but with less enthusiasm than I used to pummel Edith. I think I had enough killing for one day. I stood transfixed in the winter chill. It seemed my ghastly sickness was beginning to fade. Some relief came knowin that only myself, that mean lookin dull eyed bull in the corner and six horses would ever know what happened here. The crazy began to leave my head and my heart which had been racing through this winter annihilation started to slow while I drifted back to some sanity. It was now time to get the hell out. To fuel my escape, I clung to the idea that this was some kinda getting even for the things I never had and the shitty cards life had dealt me. Reality is, their earthly possessions and status I had coveted so much now seem meaningless. These once living, breathing human beings, full of hope, ideas, love and dreams are gone forever. What I did here accomplished exactly nothing other than stealing the life away from these good people and putting me in a bad way. In no sorta hurry, I started hiding the clues to the slaughter. I locked my arms under Mary's from behind and dragged her backwards to the death pit, her blue and white spotted bonnet slipping off her battered head. Blood was still pouring from the gashes where I had introduced daylight to her brains. She was a bit heavier than the others and it was some kinda struggle pulling her along. Since stacking the other two had taken up most of the three foot depth of the filthy makeshift grave, I just left her on top still half above ground with her two legs remaining visible outside of the stench filled ditch. I then got to cleanin up the rest of the death house best I could. There were torn bits of clothing around from all three of the girls along with Mary's bonnet so I grabbed it all, used the clean parts to mop up what I could of the red mess, tossed the heap in an empty tin bucket and threw the whole lot along with the bale stick and hatchet next to the bodies. I slid the boards back over the pit best I could not feelin the need to further cover the massacre. I knew my offence would be discovered anyhow. By now it was late in the afternoon. My mind switched to another gear which was get the hell away from here. Since the family never had visitors and nothing was stirrin next door at the neighbors, I stayed calm about the whole thing and carried on like none of it happened. Only a true lunatic could stay so composed after such a slaughter.

I took one last look around at the make shift cemetery I created and walked back to the main house. I took the path behind the barn so I wouldn't be seen by anyone passing by or the Ostranders next door. My usually faded blue overalls were by now a deep brownish color from all the dried up gore attached to them. I coolly walked into the house and headed to my room for a quick change and to bag my now useless work clothes so I could bury them away from here. It was the beginning of winter and daylight ended early so darkness was closin in. I changed off into my brown pinstriped suit and since I had nothing else, there was nothin left to gather. I did need some traveling money so I searched the house for whatever coin I could find. Blanche and Edith had nothing in their rooms aside from their purses full of girly odds and ends like makeup, talcum powder, two sterling silver hair brushes with fancy etching on the back and other assorted personal things. Since the two handbags would be easy to carry, I took them both thinkin I might be able to sell some of the stuff later. In Mary's room there was two hundred and thirty nine dollars hidden in a maple jewelry box on the bureau. No jewelry in sight. Next to the box were two bank books with more than three thousand dollars just added to each. I knew I couldn't do much with those without givin myself away so I left them where they lie thinking to myself I'd taken enough. Took one last look around and went back downstairs. I stopped dead in front of the parlor doors remembering that's where this whole mess got started. That humiliating note and my crazy being set free. One last bit of rage rose up outta me. With the heel of my Bean Boot, I kicked those two doors right in with everything I had knockin 'em clean off their hinges. Hit 'em so hard, the oak frame holding them in place split right in two. I turned around for one last look at the kitchen where the Morners sat peacefully to their last meal a few hours ago. In this thick eerie darkness, while those four bodies lie mangled just yards away, I began to understand the man inside the man. He's a product of your world. He's what you taught him to be. Fathered by the hateful streets he was educated on, mothered by the garbage cans he ate from. Never stayed in school, never had talent. He stayed poor, he stayed stupid. Tried to play by the rules you handed him while growing up in the gutter of a cruel world wrapped in some merciless coat of disdain. A heavy cloak that gave rise to this monster. For him, killing is easy, he's already dead. I opened the front door, took one wary step forward and walked off into the night.

CHAPTER TWO

The Death Blow

"Be ready for sudden death." This was the eulogy of the Reverend John Bulnes as my family were committed to the good earth. The same earth I worked for the last twenty years. Wish I knew those words sooner. Mighta been better prepared for the death blow. My name is Jesse Morner. I'm the son of a son of a farmer. Third generation of workin the land has left me quite well off. Would give it all back to see my ma, sisters and brother once more. Didn't know this time I'd be on the wrong side of the Barber dime when it turned. Bad news comes whenever it sees fit, for me it was at 8:05 three nights before last when I looked out the small four pane window by the front porch and

saw Horatio Mould the milk dealer from Rensselaer knockin. We brought our milk to him every evening where he would bottle it and send it off to the grocers. Have known him for years. He's been fair and honest with us the whole way. "Hello Harry, kinda late?" I asked. "Everything OK with you? Get you some coffee?" Horatio replied: "No sir I'm just checking up, haven't gotten my delivery from Arthur today or yesterday. Was wondering if the family was ill or something? I just knocked on their door, all the lights are down and there's no answer." "Hold on Harry, let me get my coat, we'll go take a look." Arthur was responsible for bringing the milk to market each night. He helped run the ninety acres pa had given us while I worked my own thirty eight acres a couple miles away. Guess you could say workin the land is in my blood. Hard work but it's all I know. We climbed aboard Harry's Morgan truck for the ride to our other farm. Harry didn't speak but in the flickerin light from the head lamps bouncin off the bare winter trees, I could see some kinda fear in his eyes. Being a milk dealer and salesman, Harry was usually full of conversation, tonight was different. There was an uneasy shifting back and forth in his seat, his face was expressionless, his knuckles a chalky white from his tight grip on the wheel. "Not like Arthur to miss a delivery" he said. "Yeah, better be some good God damn reason or I'm gonna hide him" Jesse exclaimed. Harry added, "Maybe the truck is down and they took the carriage out, maybe ran into some kinda trouble?" Neither of us gave thought to the worst. The worst being two days ago would be the last words I ever spoke to any of my family. *"Be ready for sudden death"* - the reverend was right. Never gave thought to it but death will smile at all of us. We'll all have a last minute we didn't know would be the last with family or a friend, God I wished I said all that needed to be said before the reaper showed his grim face. As farmers, waking up at dawn and spending all your days with your ma, brother and sisters, brings a bond and certain kinda love others wouldn't understand, after tonight, I wished I wouldn't have been afraid to show it, the things about all of them that I loved.

When we pulled up to the house, I could see everything was dark. Not a candle or lamp in any of the windows. The herd of Jerseys were clamoring in the background: "Looks like the heifers haven't been fed" Harry noted in a curious voice. I knocked; then knocked again harder. Arthur's truck was here and the carriage was parked alongside the barn so I knew they hadn't gone anywhere. Horatio, now silent, just looked at me blank faced and shrugged his shoulders. I slowly turned my key to the front door a quarter turn right releasing the latch and steadily swung the door open which cried out with a long but steady squeak. There was no other sound in the house. I immediately noticed the parlor doors in shambles on the floor. This gave me an instant and indescribable chill. Something was not right. I called upstairs, "Ma? Sis?" no answer. Grabbed a candle from the kitchen, walked upstairs and looked into each bedroom. They were all empty with the beds still made, covers neatly tucked - everything in its place. Peered into Ed's room, "Ed?" no answer. Walked back down to Horatio. "Why don't we ask Chester next door if he knows anything, maybe they're there." Chester Ostrander was a good friend, neighbor and Ma's first cousin. He and his wife did quite well on their spread. His smaller farm was directly across the street from ours and we often took time away with both of them. The main house was close enough that at night when the curtains were open, we could see in each other's windows. I gave three quick knocks. It was some time before the door opened, they were winding down for bed. "Jesse?" "Hi Chester, sorry to be knockin so late but we can't seem to find Ma and the rest, thought maybe you might know something?" "No, hadn't seen them on the farm for a couple, thought maybe they were sick. Saw the light on in Ed's room two nights ago, but no sign of the family." Chester offered to go with us up the road to the only other neighbor in the area. The home of Arthur Sharpe. I knocked on Mr. Sharpe's door. Same response, "Hadn't seen them in a few, got some lanterns in the shed, why don't we take a look around?" The four of us each grabbed a rusty red lantern, filled them with kerosene and lit 'em up. The dim yellow glow painted the hard night for at least ten feet in front and we headed back to Ma's house. Room by room we walked through the eerie silence. The sound of our footsteps on the hardwood floor and the long slow creek of door hinges being opened and closed echoed throughout the place. No fire in the stove left each room cold enough that our breath was visible in the phosphorescent light which just seemed to make the whole scene even more disturbing. There was no sign of any of them. The four of us stayed mostly silent until I spoke: "Let's try the barn." We made the short walk to the entrance and stopped in front of the slightly parted sliding doors. There's something about the prelude to unexpected horror that seems to make every muscle freeze, your heart race, breathing gets heavy and your skin turns white. I know this because in that flickering gas light was a plainly visible splash of blood on the feed box to the right. I knew we only slaughter the hogs in the back pen so the site of blood here filled my brain with indescribable fear and suspicion. Two of us slowly opened both barn doors and with lanterns in hand, raised our arms into the dark cavern. The only visible site were the horses red lit eyes set a glow behind the first stanchions. I don't know why the thought came over me, maybe from some kinda higher power but the only words I was able to speak were, "Let's try the pit." The four of us slowly walked the center aisle, our heads turning left to right as we explored the darkness looking for some kinda sign. We stopped at the first stall on the left which was usually occupied by one of our fifty or so Jerseys but was now empty. We usually let the cows graze the fields at night before bringin them in each morning for milking. The stalls were open in the back for access to the four foot wide, three foot deep manure pit which ran the length of the barn and was used to dump the cow shit into. I carefully lifted the latch on the gate and took one slow step at a time through the loose hay lying on the ground. When I reached the rear of the stall, I looked down and saw nothing. I held my lantern up in the air, looked to the right down the entire length of the barn and suddenly became perfectly still. Harry spoke up first: "Jesse? What is it?" he asked. "Not sure, somethin in the pit three stalls up." We all headed to that same stall, it was the only one with the gate slightly open. I walked in first. Didn't take more than one step when I knew hell had come to visit this farm. In that frigid air under that waning crescent moon an indescribable chill of horror came over me. Through the blackness, with my eyes now well-adjusted to the night, I saw the bottom half of two bare legs peering out of the loosely placed boards over the trench. I knew they were Mother's and I knew the death dealer had been here. I fell to my knees in some kinda silent abyss. "Jesse what's wrong?" Harry asked. "It's them." "Them?" Chester replied. "It's my ma, she's...well...she's gone." Chester spoke again in a whispered voice: "Are you sure? The night can play tricks on the light." "I'm sure" I said. He replied with, "Good lord almighty, what have you done to this family." Tears slowly rolled down my face. The woman who gave birth to me, raised me to be strong, good willed and showed me all the love in her heart, now lies here lifeless in this pool of mire. Being on the quiet side, I never had much to say, now would be no different. The three others stepped forward to see the same ghastliness I was seeing. Barely able to form any words through my quick shallow breaths, I tried to muster a little hope: "That's Ma, I just know it, maybe the others got away." Chester stepped forward to help take charge of the situation. I felt his hand on my shoulder. "Jesse, God willing, they did get away, but we gotta look, I'll do it if you can't." Chester took a few steps forward, squatted down and carefully lifted the first board covering the pit. He froze. His face in the low amber light of the incandescent lantern flame turned as white as a new fallen snow. In that moment I knew they were all gone. He slowly lowered the board back in place, turned his head and covered his now wide open mouth with his left hand. "Jesse don't look, it's all of them." The tears began to stream faster and every nerve in my body was tingling from the chill. All three men removed their hats and bowed their heads. Chester helped me to my feet. "Jesse you don't need to see this, let's go for help, there's nothing to be done now." I felt some kinda anger and madness rise up consuming my entire body. Being a rural farmer I had seen death before, human or not, but how do you describe this kind of horror? My emotions of sadness, shock and disbelief began mixing into a brew that would soon turn into anger. Didn't speak it but my only thought was, "Who could have done this?" Then, some kinda tunnel vision came about me with a hatred I've never known. The idea of a hellish revenge for the perpetrator began to consume me. Chester, with his arm around my shoulder, led me and the others down the center of the barn to the front doors. "We'll go to my house and call the sheriff." The walk across the road to Chester's place seemed like a mile though it was only a few hundred feet. Walking up the stairs of the front porch was slow and difficult. He sat me and the others at his kitchen table. I thought to myself how composed he was able to stay. He brought us a bottle: "Here have a drink." Chester poured four short glasses of Old Forester then walked towards the phone on the wall in the hallway beside the kitchen. Harry took no time in throwing the whiskey back, Mr. Sharpe soon followed. I just sat still in some kinda hellacious agony. My hand started to shake. I wrapped it around the glass and slowly brought it to my lips taking a small sip. I began to cry again in front of these grown men not thinkin I was anything less for it. I looked at the three of them and asked: "Why? My family had no enemies and were kind to everyone. What monster could have done this?" Chester returned from the hall and spoke in a confident, clear voice: "Sheriff is on his way, Jesse as God is my witness, we will find them, we will find them."

The Aftermath

By now it was 9:30 when we heard a car pull into the drive. We all stood up and walked to the door, it was Rensselaer County Sheriff William Cottrell. Chester walked out first: "Bill, we got quite a scene here, seems like somebody took all of them." "All of them?" he asked. "Yeah Jesse's whole family, they're over yonder buried in the barn." "You mean they're all dead?" "Yes as far as we can tell, all we saw was a tangled mess of bodies piled on top of each other and thrown in the manure pit. Better get some help, it's nothing one man should see on his own." "Can I use your phone?" the sheriff asked calling for two of his deputies. He then asked to take a look. "OK" Chester said, "But I gotta warn ya, I know you're the sheriff and all, but you never seen anything quite like this." Bill replied in an inquisitive voice: "OK Chester, show me." Chester took charge again: "Jesse, you and Harry stay here, Mr. Sharpe and I will take him." The two men walked the sheriff back across the road to the barn where the bodies lie. It was clear Bill was in disbelief shaking his head back and forth for what he was about to see. Once inside, he instinctively looked continually in all directions while we made our way to the massacre. Bill examined the scene and then asked Chester and Mr. Sharpe to give him a hand removing the loose boards. The three of them pulled two of the planks aside revealing a horror of unimaginable proportion. In the pool of slime became visible a stack of bodies one on top of the other disappearing into the muddy brown filth below. Mother was on top. Her head clearly beaten, one side slightly caved although still recognizable. Her dress a disgusting mix of dried blood, blackened cow shit and dirty mud. Somehow, the wicked smell of the manure pit was able to disguise the stench of death. "Jesus, what on earth" Bill spoke in a soft voice. "Good Mother Mary of God, what happened here, what insect could have done this? Better call Strope." The sheriff was referring to M.H. Strope, the Rensselaer County Coroner. Bill asked the two men to step back and walk out the way they came. "Careful, don't want to disturb any clues, I'll take it from here, let's check on Jesse, bet he could really use our help about now."

The next few hours would become nothing less than chaos as word began to spread of the grizzly slaying. The sheriff's deputies Hailligan and Poestenkill arrived just after 10:00, Coroner Strope at 10:30. Mary's brother John Schaller who lived in the City of Schenectady, twenty five miles away was also called. It would be an hour before he arrived. The sheriff sat us all down in the living room of Chester's house and began to do what any good lawman would do. Take charge of the scene and gather all the information he could. His first questions were directed towards me. "Jesse, I know this is going to be the hardest thing you've come across but I need to ask some questions, who do you think is over there?" I cleared my throat and spoke quietly but clearly. "Well, still hopin someone got away but otherwise you should expect to find Mother, Arthur, Edith," I stopped, took a deep breath and tried to find my composure. As I continued, my voice began cracking from the stress: "...My sister Blanche and our hand Ed. That's all that lived here." The sheriff went on, "Anyone have a quarrel with you or them, anyone that might still be over there in the house or other barn we should be warned of?" "No we got along fine with everyone, the new hand Ed was only with us four months but we all liked him. He was quiet, kept to himself and aside from a crush on my sister, had no beef with any of us. None that I know." The sheriff then dispatched both deputies to search the house and smaller barn to be sure the killer or killers had gone. "Fellas" he instructed them, "Take two lanterns and have a quick look around, we'll wait here twenty minutes, we don't want to walk into something we didn't expect. Whoever did this has to be some kind of animal or animals so watch yourselves." Sheriff then turned his attention to Chester. "Did you see anything unusual? Anything at all that might help? Seems unlikely there wouldn't be some commotion or noise about the place." Chester spoke calmly: "Been quiet there the past two days, thought it a little strange that I hadn't seen anyone, my wife did nod to Blanche two days ago but that was the last. The light was on in Ed's room that same night, think it was round nine, that was the only sign of anyone." "Mr. Sharpe how about you?" "No, same here, didn't see or hear anything. My wife did bring it up yesterday, asked if they were sick. She hadn't seen them around and the farm was usually busy with activity." "Jesse, when was the last you had seen any of them?" With my head hung low I replied, "Musta been four days ago when I brought a deposit by for Ma to bring to the bank." "Was there money in the house?" "Yeah Ma always kept a few dollars around for paying the deliveries and buying what we needed, mostly though, it was all kept in the bank." Bill went on in a sympathetic voice: "Jesse, when we go back over, we wouldn't think you less of a man if you stayed here." "No" I replied, "I need to know just like you do." The four men, Sheriff Cottrell, the milk dealer Horatio Mould, neighbors Arthur Sharpe, Chester Ostrander and myself all waited in silence for the deputies to return from their search of the surrounding area. Five minutes later we heard their anxious footsteps as they climbed the stairs of the front porch. "Nothing we could see boss, the door to the parlor in the house is knocked clean off the frame but no sign of anyone there or in the barns." By this time Mary's brother John who we called "Alonzo" had arrived from Schenectady with his wife. The sheriff was clear and firm in his instructions to all of us: "Now I'll need your help in uncovering all of this but it is a crime scene. We need not disturb any clues that might help get to the bottom of it so whatever we see, I need you all to follow any orders I give, Clear?" We all nodded. Chester had brought more lanterns from behind his house and the group aside from Alonzo and his wife who waited on the porch headed to the barn. "Before we pull them out, we need to take a good look around, Jesse, I want you right next to me so you can point out anything unusual. That is anything in the barn you don't usually keep there or that might belong to someone else." With lanterns in hand the group proceeded double file in a slow, somber walk to the entrance. I pointed out the splash of blood I had seen earlier on the feed box. "The blood must be from one of them" I exclaimed, "No reason it should be here." As an entire group we walked the center aisle of the barn. Mr. Sharpe stopped and pointed over to the foot of a horse stanchion where he noticed another bloodstain and clump of black hair matted together: "Looks like here is where one of them dropped" he proclaimed. The sheriff took a closer look while the deputies began to write feverishly in their notebooks taking in all of what was said and discovered. The sheriff directed us to split into three groups and search each stall. This went on for fifteen minutes, mostly in silence other than the sound in the background of the fifty or so cows returning to the barn bellowing out their discomfort for not being fed. After examining every corner of every stall, myself and the others gathered in the center of the barn. I handed over a gold pocket watch found in the first stall. "This was my brother's, Pa had left it to him." The sheriff opened the soiled round hinged cover and noted it had stopped ticking at 5:10. "Anyone find anything else?" he asked, there was no reply. "Guess we better get to it then. Strope I'll turn this over to you, how do you want to go about it?" The coroner, having spent his life amongst the dead, seemed unfettered by the call to remove the bodies. "I'll need the three strongest" he said. "We will bring 'em out one by one and let the sheriff get a good look at each as there might be some hint to what occurred. Jesse, you're to wait here, there's no discussion about that." The serenity of the nearby cows chewing their cud and whisking their tales, while four men moved fervently to uncover mangled limbs and bloodied bodies in the flickering feeble rays of yellow lantern light, just seemed to add more gloom and horror to the shocking scene. By this time Mary's brother

Alonzo and his wife had entered and were watching over the proceedings, his wife crying out: "Heavens Alonzo, do not look." The first body which was Mother's, was carefully lifted from the muck. Her face was barely recognizable and her head had three large gashes clearly caused by the blade of an axe or hatchet. There were three other similar wounds on her nearly naked body which by this time was stiff as rigor mortis had set in. She must have been twenty pounds heavier with all of the mud and excrement from the pit stuck to it. "Jesse, turn your head" one of the men spoke as the four carried her body outside and laid it on the frozen winter ground. The second body in the pile of gore which was lying directly underneath Mother's was Edith. Deputy Hailligan noted out loud how her arms were still crossed in front of her face, the right one clearly broken. "She must have tried to block them and passed just like that." Edith's head was nearly decapitated. Her wounds far worse than the others. There were multiple gashes from a hatchet covering her nearly naked body and her torso was pierced a dozen or so times with a sharp object. As she was carried out, Coroner Strope placed his hand underneath the back of the head to hold it in place, there was little keeping it attached. Her remains were placed beside Mother's. By this time, the men were beginning to cough and gasp from the stench of the rotting corpses combined with the days old animal refuge. Each had removed a handkerchief from their pockets and had tied them tightly around their mouths and noses to make the smell of rotting flesh more bearable. Underneath Edith's body was Blanche. Hers was the most recognizable. Half naked and slightly bloodied, her face and head seemed untouched aside from bruises along her left cheek. The only wound that appeared visible was a stab wound to her left side. Before lifting her body, the four men turned and looked at each other. Without speaking a word, it was obvious they all thought the same thing: "She's the last, where are the others?" I was quick to notice the same. From my well of despair, rose a glimmer of hope, not more than the size if a candle flame. Maybe my brother had escaped the carnage. The sheriff spoke up, "Jesse, he's not here," referring to Arthur. "Anyplace he might have run to? Another barn or shed in the fields?" "Not sure" I replied, "No place out here to hide, unless he just ran to Snyder's Lake or Averill Park. Seems we would have heard from him by now." That thought extinguished the dwindling flicker of hope I had held on to. I broke down again and began to sob softly as the body of my youngest sister Blanche was carried out. Coroner Strope took it upon himself to cover their mutilated forms with wool horse blankets from the barn. Sheriff then took control again. Agreeing with me that they would have heard something from Arthur by now, he instructed the group to form parties of three, each to grab a lantern and to walk the night. "We're missing two, Arthur and the farmhand Ed" he explained. At this time, no thought was given to either of them being involved in the atrocity so all energy was devoted to finding them. Dead or alive. In the cold black night of December 13th, 1911, a half dozen parties of three men each, dotted the Defreestville countryside with dim points of yellow light from hand held lanterns as they scoured the darkness. For three hours every room, shed, chicken coop and corner of the ninety acres was explored. Nothing, not a clue to their whereabouts or the crime was discovered until the sheriff and his deputies re-entered the main house. Aside from the parlor doors being off their hinges, nothing appeared out of the ordinary. No sign of struggle, nothing else was broken and it appeared nothing was taken. The sheriff addressed the group: "Strange, if it was robbery, why wouldn't they grab the kitchen silver or any other valuables in the parlor, surely they had the time." He then called for more lanterns and the help of deputies Hailligan and Poestenkill to search the house in detail. It was deputy Halligan to be the first to spot it: "Look, there, on the banister" it was a clear blood stain in the shape of a small palm print. The clue was at the top of the stairs directly across from the farmhand Ed's room. The sheriff opened a discussion with his deputies: "Arthur and the hand are both missing, might be they were both in on it?" Being a fine lawman, the good sheriff knew he had to explore any and all possibilities. Even if that meant something as grotesque as Arthur Morner being involved. By now it was three in the morning. All of the make shift search parties had returned and gathered in front of the house, each reporting back they had found nothing. It was decided by the sheriff to return to the barn and uncover the entire pit. We started where the first three were found thinkin the bodies of the other two might be buried further below. Deputy Hailligan raised a shovel and with all his strength, slammed it deep into the muddy pit, the rounded point quickly being met with clear resistance. He wiggled the blade of the shovel back and forth, pushed the end of the handle down and brought to the surface a tin bucket. "Stop!" the sheriff said excitedly, "Careful, I can see it's packed with something." The deputy slowly lifted the bucket and gently slid it off the end of the shovel placing it in the stall. The sheriff wearing a pair of old work gloves he grabbed from a shelf in the barn removed the solid mass from inside. It was clear they were the bloody remnants of clothing worn by my family. "Looks like they tried to hide everything here" the sheriff exclaimed while carefully examining the contents. As he spread apart the mass of hardened cloth, I immediately recognized the bonnet Mother usually wore. A quick painful exhale preceded my words: "That's Ma's." The deputy then returned with shovel in hand to the pit. He turned back again to the stall, this time dropping a blood stained hatchet. "There's a bale stick down here too" he reported in a somewhat energized voice. The sheriff, normally composed, just shook his head: "This was clearly the work of an insane man or men, those poor kids didn't have a chance, I shudder to think what they must have gone through." After more excavating, the deputy was sure there was nothing else in that spot. Sheriff Cottrell, deputy Poestenkill and myself also grabbed shovels and began digging along the entire length of the pit, some thirty feet or so. Four shovels and four men kept hacking away at the muddy mess as the morning light began to spill into the windows of the barn giving a clearer view of the interior. I stopped for a breath and walked back to the center aisle. That's when I noticed the first hint to Arthur's whereabouts. Being a farmer is my life's work. I know every tool, cart, carriage, saddle, strap, every inch of the barn and the entire property. "Musta missed it the dark, but there's something not right here." I called the other three over and pointed to the ground in front of the stall that housed one of the horses. The floor of the barn was constructed of twelve inch by ten foot oak planks. After years of trampling by human feet, cattle and farm equipment, the boards had turned into what looked to be one solid mass. Each crack, seam and crevice filled in with dirt and mud from the traffic. I noticed right away two of the boards in front of the first stall had been disturbed. The wood around the nails holding them in place was clearly chipped away leaving a fresh light brown color. The normally rusty heads of the nails were now showing some of their original steel grey. The two deputies each grabbed a claw hammer hanging on the wall in the front of the barn and began to carefully pry up the dozen or so nails implanted in the boards. I handed the sheriff a crow bar and we anxiously awaited the deputies task of pulling the steel pegs. "Jesse, stand back, I'll take care of this" Bill instructed. With a firm hard shove between the two now loosened floorboards, the sheriff drove the ten pound steel crowbar in the small gap created from removing the nails. At 9 AM on the morning of the 14th, the remaining mystery had almost been solved. Underneath the boards, covered in loosely packed earth, were the remains of my brother. The three lawmen stared in silence while I quietly removed myself from the barn. I had already prepared myself for this discovery and had hardened all emotions. Like the bodies of the rest, Arthur's form was frightfully mutilated. The rear part of his skull had been crushed, his throat had been cut, apparently with a razor or knife, and one of his ears was nearly severed. His face was covered with small cuts and scrapes. It was thought from these facial injuries that the body had been dragged along the floor, face down, to the spot where it was hidden beneath the floor. Expecting to find the farmhand Ed in a similar fashion, the search of the barn continued. Each floorboard, loft and stall were carefully examined for any sign of abnormality. None were found. Still thinking the farmhand a victim, another daylight search of the property was ordered by Sheriff Cottrell. The three watering ponds were dragged for the missing body, the two wells drained and every inch of the farm examined for something out of the ordinary. Still no sign. This is when Sheriff Cottrell began to form a mental picture of the massacre. He called me over, "Jesse, what do you know of this Ed fellow?" "Not much other than what the Empire Agency in Albany had told Arthur. That's how he came to us. Art said nothin out of the ordinary. Seemed like a good fellow, did his work, kept to himself." "Anything else?" he asked. "Art said he was kind around the girls but come to think of it, he did mention a rather unusual interest he mighta had in Blanche." "Unusual interest?" "Yeah, maybe some kinda crush." The sheriff at this time was noting everything. I knew Bill quite well. He was a good sheriff. I was glad he would be on the case. By this time, all of the men were well exhausted. The physical and mental anguish left us all without words. Bill outstretched his arm and put his hand on my shoulder: "Jesse, why don't you try and get some rest, we'll wake you if we come across anything." Of course sleep was not to come for some time. What sleep that did arrive was filled with dreams of my brother and sisters when we were kids. We had no clue then to the perverse world around us or did we care. Our only problem was trying to figure out which fishin spot at Miller's pond we would each claim or who had rights to the best sittin branch in the big apple tree. Our days were filled with an insatiable curiosity for all things and the invention of responsibility had not yet been introduced to our young minds. These were days without any sense of the hour only interrupted by the occasional trip back to the house for a glass of milk, bandaging of a scraped knee or until Ma called us in at sundown. This was the time that made us. The school plays, stray cats and dogs we brought home, games of hoop and stick and the endless parade of practical jokes we played during our chores. No one told us those days would end but I wish they had, I would have taken them to bed each night with a different point of view. My mother, brother and sisters are gone now but each one in their own way still survive in the memories I take with me as I continue along my own journey. Those memories sometimes appear in the divided light of the sun disappearing behind the fields we played in when we were kids. Our footprints there are long gone but I somehow still see them. I will miss my family and regret not telling them all the things...we'll, you know, just telling them.

Goodbye

The morning of the 17th, I rose before dawn. I knew today would be the beginning of putting this behind. Today is the day my family is to be buried. The undertaker, William J. Rockefeller had decided it best to prepare the bodies here on the farm and lay them out in the parlor for final viewing. Before Rockefeller did his work, Coroner Strope did a full examination of each family member and was preparing his report for the sheriff. The good undertaker used all of his skill in making my family presentable. Their heads were wrapped in bright white cotton to conceal their wounds and each were dressed in their Sunday clothes. Mother in a black gown that wrapped tightly around her neck and a grey button down over coat left open, Edith in her purple and blue pleated dress also buttoned to her neck, Blanche in her favorite lily patterned blue dress with one inch lace around the collar. Arthur in his black Sunday suit. Mother and the girls each rest in shiny white caskets lined in dark pink satin, Arthur's was a clean light brown oak lined in tan suede. All four with matching brushed silver handles. The bodies were to be buried at the Blooming Grove Cemetery and the funeral was set for 12:00. It was scarcely daylight and the first sliver of orange sun had just appeared over the hills when mourners began to arrive at the farm. By 8:00, every road leading to the surreal scene was congested with automobiles, vehicles of all kinds and pedestrians. By 9:00, there were more than 5,000 people at the house, some morbidly exploring the barn. There was a profusion of flowers sent by friends and neighbors with many bringing baskets of food. The gathering almost resembled a picnic. Just before 9:30, Mr. Rockefeller appeared at the front door of the house which had remained locked announcing that all that wished could view the bodies. There was a wild rush for the door. Sheriff Cottrell, his deputies and twelve assistants managed to form the pack into a line. Mourners passed through the front of the parlor and exited at the rear of the house. After two somber hours, the front doors were ordered closed. Some of the women fainted in the crush to get a final glimpse. The sheriff then instructed the crowd outside to make way for the four horse-drawn hearses that were to carry the coffins three miles to the cemetery. The shimmering black carriages were of the finest workmanship I had ever seen. The rear cabin supported by four hand-turned fluted pillars on each corner, oversized windows adorned in gold satin curtains and hand carvings of all shapes and sizes dressed the side skirts. The four chariots were each drawn by a pair of Clydesdales with a single driver perched in front, his black top hat peering above the whole collection. It was quite an honorable site. One by one, myself, Mother's cousin Chester and two of her brothers Alonzo and Johannes each carried the coffins by their sculpted silver handles to the waiting caravan. Quickly the mass of people began to part clearing the way for the procession. I didn't think it possible for such a large crowd to be so silent that you could still here a single croaking bullfrog down by the pond. The hearses then began to make their way through the countryside, the journey slowed considerably by an assortment of carriages, wagons and automobiles which blocked the surrounding muddy roads fifteen miles in all directions. When we finally arrived at the cemetery, four generations of my family gathered hand-in-hand for the service which finally began at 1:30. My grandmother, my aunts, uncles and my son Clifford, Mother's only grandchild were all here. Reverend John Bulnes, pastor of the Blooming Grove Reformed Church performed the eulogy. Under a frigid December sky with the mixed sound of hushed sobbing and low spoken threats against the killer in the background, the reverend began his sermon. I kept my head up, the shock from this horrendous misfortune had mostly been swallowed and I thought nothing other than the loneliness ahead. Reverend Bulnes started with words that would stay with me for the rest of my life: *"Be ready for sudden death."* I immediately thought how wrong I was to have overlooked such a relevant thought my whole life. I would not have drowned myself in the sentiment but would have quietly celebrated each day I had with my mother, brother and sisters. At the time, I would have embraced what I didn't know was going to be my last summer with them a few months before. While the bodies were lowered to their final resting place, the congregation began to recite the Christian Endeavor benediction followed by a quartet which sang "Lead Kindly Light." The entire crowd remained at the cemetery while the graves were covered. I stood warmed by the outpouring of affection I received. Knowing this many people had come to pay their respects to my family, only reaffirmed the love this community had for each of them. A love they will carry with them for eternity. Lord knows I will miss them. The reverend went on to finish with words of enlightenment for all of us:

"Set thy house in order, for you do not know when he comes."

CHAPTER THREE

Catch-em

The freshly turned earth in the Blooming Grove Cemetery was still damp while I stared motionless at the four neatly carved plots. These were not strangers buried beneath. I recalled the three days earlier and the events that took place at the Morner farm while trying to solve this crime. The day after the murders, headlines were already spreading faster than the country gossip: "Find The Italian", "Where's The Death Dealer?" Damn I only hope these newspaper men don't muddy the water with their wild stories of an axe wielding madman roaming the countryside. Residents here are already on edge thinking a killer is still lurking in the vicinity. My name is William L. Cottrell, Sheriff of Rensselaer County. There's an intense bitterness for me about these murders and I've taken it personally. The Morners were friends and fine people unworthy of an ending like this. Being a rural sheriff, I've seen car wrecks, mangled bodies, arms and legs shredded by farm machinery and every kind of gunshot wound you can think of. These killings top them all, especially since they were no accident. Right now, I have to get past my sympathy for Jesse and the others and get down to the business of solving this case. Since he has not shown himself at the farm, dead or alive, my only logical conclusion is that we are looking for an Italian immigrant named Edward Donato aka "Edward Di Donato" aka "Dennis." Several theories have been suggested to who the killer or killers were and perhaps Donato was actually a victim, but my instinct and all the facts were pointing to the Italian. If Donato was the assailant, I still didn't know his mindset. Was this an isolated event or would he kill again? For now, my energy and resources were devoted to locating him. He now had a good seventy two hours on us and the man is most likely miles away by now, possibly already at sea. Around midday on the afternoon we removed Arthur Morner from under the floor of the barn, I called in detective William A. Humphrey of the New York Central Railroad in Utica. He had two of the finest bloodhounds in the northeast. If this madman had tried to escape the area, they were sure to track him. I have known Humphrey for some time, his dogs were the best I've ever seen. They are born finders of lost things. For humans, tracking is a learned skill brought on by necessity, for these hounds it's ingrained in their blood. They have been obsessed with scent for more than a hundred generations. Perfect tracking machines. Their bloodlines can be traced back to 700 AD when they were bred as hunters in Belgium. Humphrey told me most bloodhounds hunt in packs and follow a few lead dogs, these two "Chief" and "General" tried to lead the bunch even when they were pups. I'm sure they'll tell us if Donato fled. The three arrived in Troy on the 2:15 from Utica. I summonsed deputies

Hailligan and Poestenkill who were closest to the case to meet us at the farm and we went to it. The first step was finding something of Donato's with scent. To our luck, he had left behind a brown fedora and denim overalls hanging in his closet which I had earlier instructed Jesse and the deputies not to touch so any scent left behind would not be disturbed. The dogs were brought upstairs to the farmhand's bedroom and led to the leftover garments. Tails began wagging and ears perked up. This is what these animals lived for and they showed it. It was like watching a ten year old light up on Christmas morning. Through flared black nostrils they both began quick sporadic sniffs of the clothing in an attempt to locate any hint of Donato. The pair quickly became even more excited and it was obvious their senses had discovered his smell. Humprey then uttered two words which he quickly repeated twice: "Go find, go find." With 'v' shaped jowls nearly touching the ground and heads swinging side to side snatching up the killers aroma, the two canine sleuths turned and darted down the stairway. Their noses still working the air, they hurriedly exited the house jumping over both steps to the front porch and headed directly towards the barn, the doors of which had been shut so not to confuse the hunt. With yelps of exultation which must have been heard for miles, the persistent hounds circled the building twice. This told us the scent was still fresh. Chief and General then headed east down the packed dirt road towards Averill Park. I climbed in my car and the deputies in theirs. The dogs were so adamant about their job, we had a hard time keeping up. This was like watching a master painter perform his craft right in front of you. It was astounding. For miles the pair did not waiver. Humphrey himself had a hard time keeping up while his short somewhat bow-legged stride seemed to slow him down. His worn out breath further strained by the occasional rally cry of "get 'em boys, get 'em" which was amplified as it echoed through the towering white pines on both sides of the road. This was good news. Wherever this man had fled, we were on him. Thanks to the astonishing speed of the canine detectives, we covered six miles in just over one hour and landed at the trolley tracks of the New England Railway in West Sand Lake. This was a bit concerning. If the man boarded a trolley here, we were sure to lose the trail. I questioned the station agent on duty who offered little information but told us the 2nd shift conductor, Bob Allen, who was also working the night of the murder would be arriving at 4:00. He explained that Mr. Allen was quite sharp and would be able to help with any details had the culprit boarded here. Sure enough at precisely 4 PM we had our first clue to Donato's path. Mr. Allen stated that an Italian looking man matching the fugitive's description had indeed climbed aboard the train here late Tuesday evening but was put off at Snyder's lake. "The fella seemed a bit agitated and worn from what musta been a long walk, when I asked him for fare, he only had a nickel in his pocket so I had no choice but to put him off at the next stop which was Snyder's." I suspected Donato had lifted some cash from the Morner farm so at first, only having a five cent piece didn't make sense. After further contemplation, I figured Donato must be of some intelligence. Waving a handful of cash in front of the conductor, or having to pull it from some concealed area on his person, might only lead to suspicion, so it would only make sense that he chose to exit at Snyder's knowing the line didn't go much further. To continue the search, we bordered the trolley here in West Sand Lake, hounds in tow, for the short ride to the Snyder's Lake station. When we exited the trolley there, Humphrey began zigzagging Chief and General in the area of the station platform. To our amazement these wonderful dogs immediately began crying out with tails waving back and forth. It was clear they had rejoined the scent. We followed the pair again for thirty minutes and came to the entrance of a large whitewashed horse barn just outside of Troy. The property belonged to Dr. E.J. Knauf who graciously gave permission to search the premises. Upon entering, it was clear from the dogs reaction the dankness of the barn was unable to mask the lingering spirit of Donato and it was obvious he had spent the night of the killings here. There were no clues or materiel evidence present so we exited the barn and followed the dogs who quickly headed north, apparently back on the trail. After a brief walk, Chief and General slowly pulled up on the road to Albia just outside of Troy and began a "circle search." This happens when they become confused or lose the smell of their prey so they begin to wander aimlessly in tight circles. We gave them a few minutes to walk the area but nothing. I could only conclude the scent was lost. Donato must have hitched a ride from here. This was good and bad news. We had in fact been on the killers trail but no other evidence was to be collected and it appeared we were back to the beginning in our search for this monster.

The next morning proved to be a difficult one. Although the hounds convinced me Donato had fled, I had to put to rest speculation that he was actually a victim not the killer and that robbery was the true motive. This idea was presented with little merit. Too many valuables were left behind. Recent deposits of more than $3,000 were in each of two bankbooks and a number of other items of considerable worth were left throughout the house. Sixty dollars in cash was also found in the top drawer of Mary's burrow. This was determined to be payment from Horatio Mould for a milk delivery the night before the murders. I ordered another search of the property and every floorboard in the barn to be removed in the event Donato's body was buried beneath. There was also talk that Jesse Morner might be in on the crime. He was to inherit a substantial amount of land and money so some in the community suggested he had more motive than anyone to commit the felony. It sickened me to think I had to pursue him but the good people of Rensselaer elected me to do a job and I had to perform it to the best of my ability. I had to be thorough and remain impartial, that's a lawman's job. I assigned deputy Poestenkill the task of taking a statement from Jesse. He questioned him in the sitting room of the farmhouse. It's the job of a good officer to rattle a potential suspect and although he was a friend, Jesse was put through the 3rd degree. Deputy Poestenkill did the best he could to be affable about it. Questions were hurled at Jesse from every angle as far back to when his father Conrad died. He was then asked why he suggested looking under the manure pit when they first arrived at the barn the night after the murders. "I know every inch of this property" he explained, "If someone were to hide anything out of site, that was the only logical place." Deputy Poestenkill went on asking Jesse if he had been friendly with Donato and what his thoughts were on inheriting the whole lot to which he replied: "Never crossed my mind about the money or land and I knew Donato only as an employee, we were not friendly other than the usual working relationship." The deputy reported to me that Jesse seemed upset but offered no "tells" in his demeanor to suggest he was hiding something. Jesse Morner was a very quiet, even tempered man and the assault on his integrity clearly rattled him. The neighbors and community also resented the only surviving family member being a possible suspect but no stone was to be left unturned. Although Jesse's involvement was not to be completely dismissed, attention was then turned elsewhere. In addition to ordering every floorboard in the barn being pulled, I brought in William T.

Powers, a finger print expert from the State Prison Department who did a complete canvassing of the area. After three hours, all men involved in the investigation gathered in the kitchen of the farmhouse along with detectives Cirillo and Talbot from Troy. Assistant District Attorney Quillinan was also present. The four shared their findings along with any physical evidence. Aside from the results of Coroner Strope's autopsy report which should arrive in three days, I documented for the record what was collected to date:

1. William Powers, finger print expert, discovered a clear thumb print left in blood four feet from the floor on the 3rd pillar to the right of the entrance to the main barn. A large piece of the beam was cut away and the print held as evidence.

2. A bloody palm print was found on the banister directly across the hall from Edward Donato's bedroom.

3. Nine splashes of blood raging in size from a single drop to a thumb nail were found on a feed trough to the right side of the entrance to the barn. It is undetermined as to who the blood belonged to.

4. A clump of black matted hair three inches in length was found near the horse stanchion across from the 4th stall on the left side of the barn. The color of which, matching that of Edith Morner.

5. Drag marks of twelve feet and six inches in length were visible leading from the location of the three corpses discovered in the manure pit to considerable pools of dried blood in front of the 4th stall on the left side of the barn, the largest pool being three feet in diameter. This would indicate these victims were dropped in front of the stall.

6. A hatchet and bale stick were found buried with the victims in the manure pit. The handle of the hatchet being constructed of a smooth oak, did not hold prints and none were found.

7. A hand written letter was found on the desk in Edward Donato's bedroom. The letter was addressed to his father at 323 Water Street, Springfield, Massachusetts. The letter asked that he be sent tickets so he could go to Tripoli and "fight Africans." The letter further stated, "If you don't send me the money, I go to consul in NY and tell them I'm a soldier and he will see to send me to Italy."

8. Reported missing by Jesse Morner were two paisley patterned woman's purses, one red, the other green and an estimated two to three hundred dollars in cash.

9. The doors to the parlor had been smashed in and were completely off their frame. A clear boot mark found on the exterior right side door, indicates the panels were kicked in with considerable force. Nothing else in the house was disturbed.

10. A hand written note was found on the piano in the parlor that read: "Italian meat and

American made sausage imported from Rome Italy."

The origin of this note proved to be of some disagreement between DA Quillinan and myself. Quillinan was under the impression the note was *not* written by Donato. The handwriting did not appear to match that of the letter found in his bedroom which was clearly written by his hand. The speculation was it had been penned by one of the Morner's. I had also gathered statements from friends, neighbors and family in order to help establish a timeline to the murders. There was little pertinent information and I noted as follows:

1. Chester Ostrander (neighbor from directly across the street) stated he saw Donato lingering around the barn doors at approximately 12 PM on Tuesday the 12th. One hour later he saw Edith Morner walking towards the barn. He further stated he saw a light on in Donato's room that same evening at approximately 9 PM.

2. At approximately 3:30 PM on Monday the 11th, a local seamstress, Mrs. Margaret McCann, stated Donato had went to her home to have trousers mended. They were ripped from the knee down on the right leg. She recalled the man was wearing a brown pinstripe suit. Mrs. McCann had no further information to offer on his state of mind other than: "Nothing seemed out of the ordinary."

3. Mrs. Arthur Sharpe, neighbor from one hundred yards west, stated she had commented to her husband on the 13th that there had not been any movement on the Morner farm for two days and asked her husband if he thought the family were sick.

4. John Schaller (aka Alonzo), Mary's brother from Schenectady was asked what he knew of Donato and stated: "The man seemed to be alright and got along OK with the women." He was then asked, "Was your sister in the habit of keeping money around?" He replied, "Yes, I think she always had one or two hundred dollars in the house."

Aside from additional clues in the final autopsy report, we have little to go on and my opinion still remains Edward Dennis Donato is the man we should be looking for.

The Aftermath

After the funeral, neighbors came to help on the Morner farm doing everything they could to assist Jesse in carrying on the necessary chores. The entire country began to read about the case as newspaper accounts spread around the nation. The Governor of New York, John Alden Dix, also took interest. Dix issued a statement to the press offering a $2,000 reward for "the capture of the perpetrators of this heinous crime." The Rensselaer County Board of Supervisors then added an additional $1,000 in reward money followed by Jesse Morner contributing another $500 making the total prize $3,500. Governor Dix in his press release further added: "I feel very keenly about the situation and believe every effort should be made by authorities to bring the assassin to justice. I would have offered a larger award if it were in my power, however, Attorney General Carmody informed me that the now $3,000 award from the state and county, is the maximum allowed." When asked about distributing tax payer money in this manner, the governor cited previous precedents as follows: "Governor Flower in 1892 offered a reward of $2,500 for the capture of Thomas O'Brian who was charged with killing a prominent Albanian. Governor Morton offered a $1,000 award in April 1895 for the apprehension of Oliver Curtis Perry, the noted train robber who is at present confined in the State Hospital for the Criminally Insane at Dannemora. A similar amount was offered by Governor Black in 1898 for the return to the Sheriff of Sullivan County of a Wallace J. Christian who had escaped custody there."

Most residents of Rensselaer County agreed with our pursuit of Donato as the killer but the community's own gossip machine presented alternate theories. There were still a few that insisted Jesse Morner had been involved in the deaths. Notably, two private detectives, Richard J. Reilly and Frank Mcdermott a former

Troy policeman who were pursuing their own investigation. The two claimed Jesse had recently purchased a pair of white gloves that he later stated were missing, thus insinuating they were used somehow in the crime. They attempted to rattle Jesse further by pointing to the fact the ninety acres at 33 Morner Road were now all his and made him one of the wealthiest farmers in the county. It was a matter of record that Jesse also inherited exactly $12,255.38. $2,700.00 from Mary, $4,299.15 from Arthur, $3,332.58 from Edith and $1,923.65 from Blanche. Fueled only by speculation, the two detectives decided to bring Jesse before District Attorney Abbot H. Jones for questioning. Jesse resisted and pulled a revolver on the two men who were ultimately able to subdue him and place him in their car. The DA questioned Jesse for two hours but he did not waiver. Jesse even invited myself and my deputies to search his home which I quickly stated wouldn't be necessary. Realizing this was some kind of wild goose chase, the DA ordered his release. The usually reserved Jesse, then broke out in an uncharacteristic outburst first aimed at me. "How long is this gonna go on?" he asked angrily. I explained that I did not order the private detectives to seek him out and apologized for their actions. Jesse again raised his voice: "To think that anybody should think that I had anything to do with that horrible crime is almost more than I can stand, the grief over losing my mother, sisters and brother is great enough but why should I be accused of this." Jesse was right to bring shame down on them.

The following day, the autopsy report arrived from Coroner Strope. Strope had put together a short summary of his findings which read: "Aside from all four victims displaying small abrasions and contusions, cause of death was as follows: Mary Morner died from blunt force trauma caused by a six inch dull blade matching the measurements, width and length, of the hatchet found at the scene. She was struck three times in the skull and three times in the upper torso. Edith Morner died from blunt force trauma to the head. She was struck once on the left side of her skull and once in the neck by a six inch dull blade matching the measurements, width and length, of the hatchet found at the scene. Her head was nearly decapitated from the hatchet blow to the neck which resulted in considerable blood loss. Also contributing to her blood loss were fifteen stab wounds to the torso with a three inch wide pointed circular object of considerable length which matched the width of the bale stick found at the scene. She sustained an additional nine wounds to the upper torso from the aforementioned hatchet which also resulted in a complete fracture of the right forearm four inches below the elbow. Arthur Morner died from a knife wound to the front of his throat leaving an unrecoverable gash of five and one quarter inches in length and two inches in depth. The back of his skull was fractured from a blow with a long narrow object, the width of the wound, matching that of the bale stick found at the scene. Blanche Morner died from a single stab wound to her left side by a five inch long, two inch wide blade which penetrated her torso above the fourth rib piercing her heart by exactly one half inch." The report went on to state: "Bruises were found to cover the entire circumference of both wrists and the back of each hand indicating Blanche Morner was restrained against a hard surface. This type of contusion further indicates there was considerable resistance by the girl. This is also relevant to the discovery that Blanche Morner's virtue had been taken." This last bit was the most convincing piece of evidence I believe we had and might point to a clear motive. Donato must have had some type of relationship or affection for the girl. Knowing the family was a close-knit unit, I don't believe anything consensual was going on between the two as the family would be aware. It was hinted by friends and family that Donato did indeed have a significant interest in the girl, therefore I must conclude from the evidence, she was taken against her will. Aside from an argument of undetermined origin with the family, I can think of no other seed to set forth the event that occurred on Decemeber 12th than a reaction of some sort by Donato to his apparent infatuation with the girl. This led to a possible argument with one or all of the family members resulting in their deaths. It is further noted that the manner in which each victim was slain, indicates they fell individually, most likely unnoticed by the others. It is the conclusion of this officer, that Edward Dennis Donato was the perpetrator of this crime and that he acted alone. It is further suggested, that a nationwide bulletin be presented for the capture of this dangerous fugitive. Word should also be sent overseas with a focus on all Italian ports of entry to be on the lookout for the man's arrival.

With no sign Donato is still in the area or any conclusive evidence pointing to another possible suspect, my attention now turned to Hudson and Springfield where the fugitive once lived. There were regular trains running from Troy and Albany to both cities allowing him an easy escape. We started in Hudson. Mr. Vincent, manager of the Empire Employment Agency in Albany, was able to offer some background information which told us Donato previously lived there and provided his old address. Hudson Police Chief Lane was instructed to help with the investigation and their department spread word to local residents and businesses asking for any information related to the Italian. The next firm piece of evidence came when I questioned one of Lane's men, Officer Martin. The officer stated: "At around 5 AM Wednesday morning the 13th, I ran into Donato on Columbia Street. I've known him for more than two years. It was him. His eyes were bloodshot and he was wearing a brown pinstripe suit and tan wool overcoat. He asked about getting a train to Pittsfield. When I told him it would be a few hours before the next, he said he would go visit a friend." No further details to who the friend might be were offered but it seemed we were again on the trail. We then visited Donato's previous Hudson address. His former roommate Pasquale Mele still lived at that location. Mr. Mele was cooperative and stated: "I had not seen Ed for some time, last I heard, he was livin in Springfield with his pa." Mele seemed a bit nervous. He fidgeted with a pack of Camel's resting on the table in front of him. Chief Lane previously told me Mele had "quite a background on the wrong side." This raised my suspicion but we were unable to find any hard evidence in the apartment and Mr. Mele had nothing else to offer. The fact that he *did not ask why* we were looking for Donato, led me to suspect he had seen his old roommate recently and was withholding information. Mele was not the sort to be forthcoming. The next tip came from Front Street saloon keeper Charles Carosio who stated: "I saw him in my place at around midnight on Wednesday. I knew the man when he had lived here; he was trying to stay out of sight and hung mostly around the back room. We exchanged a few words when he approached the bar and asked 'Hello, don't you know me?' I replied yeah, you're Ed. Seemed like he just wanted to know if he had been noticed. He just turned and walked out." Later that same afternoon, Hudson police chief Lane informed me he had in custody an Antonio Renear who claimed Donato stayed with him on the night of the 13th. I questioned the witness who stated: "I knew Ed for a couple of years and we were roommates for a while. I ran into him in front of Charlie's place. He seemed out of sorts and asked about trains going to Pittsfield. He looked like he hadn't slept so I offered him my sofa. I know nothing about what you say he done. I mighta bent the law a bit but man, if I knew he was involved in something like that,

I would have spoken to the law." Mr. Ranear then described a tan wool overcoat and brown suit the man was wearing. We were now sure the killer had passed through here so I sent two deputies to search the roads between our location and Pittsfield where he was likely to have traveled next. We also visited the Hudson terminal of the New York Central Railroad. The agent there stated he sold a man fitting Donato's description a ticket to Pittsfield. Station agents and conductors at both ends of the line were questioned but we gathered no new information. I'm sure the Italian is on the move and has left this area. Our only chance at an arrest may come from Pittsfield or possibly Springfield. I sent word ahead to the Berkshire County Sheriff in Massachusetts for his cooperation to which he replied: "Been following this case from the beginning, we've all been on alert here. If that greasy animal shows his face, we'll take him." Despite the good sheriff's enthusiasm and knowing Donato now had a good five day start on us, I fear the trail is cold. We continued our efforts in Pittsfield where we found no clues then on to Springfield where we located his father who still lived at 323 Water Street, the address on the letter found in Dontao's bedroom. Mr. Donato dressed in worn but well-kept wool trousers and matching shirt topped off with a tweed coppola spoke broken English but was quite capable of understanding our questions. I offered him a seat and explained in detail why we were here. Mr. Donato with a scared worried look on his face slowly cupped his aged hand over his oval shaped open mouth, paused to gather his thoughts then spoke in a stiff Italian accent. "I have not seen my boy in a year. He said he was going to the country, now you tell me my son has done something like this? He's a good boy; he does not have that in him." The old man was visibly shaken and I believe he did not know of the murders but probably had seen his son afterwards. I needed to rattle him a bit to be sure. "Mr. Dontao if you have any information please tell us. If your boy did commit this ghastly crime, he is ill, it's important to tell us what you know so we can stop it from happening again. If you hide anything, you will be sent back to Italy and might even be charged with obstruction, do you know what that is sir?" I slammed my hand on the table for effect. "It means you knew something that could help us solve this but *did not* tell us." The frightened father began to take slow deep breaths, his eyes teared up and he looked right at me: "I know nothing of this other than I won't see my boy again." He wept out loud: "Please leave me, if you find my son..." he stopped there and left the room. I couldn't help feel for the man but I also felt for the Morners who were given no choice in their fate. I don't think Donato would have passed through here without seeing his kin and I'm sure his father knows where he's headed but there is no chance he would talk. These Italians stick together with their unspoken code of silence which sticks even harder when it's your own blood. I believe the man is most likely on his way overseas. Without some miracle in the distance, this fugitive is not likely to be caught.

In the days to come, suspects in cities all over the northeast who fit the description of Donato were detained, none proving to be the killer. The newspaper accounts were noted to our investigation.

Buffalo, New York
December 15th, 1911
"A man fitting the description of Edward Donato who is believed to be the killer of Mrs. Conrad Morner and her family was wandering the streets near the Franklin Street rail station in Lackawanna at 3 AM. Anthony Mori was taken into custody by Chief Regan and was ordered held by Judge Nash. He was later released on lack of evidence."

Coxsackie, New York
December 16th, 1911
"Samuel Raymond was arrested in Coxsackie last night carrying a letter addressed to Ed Donato. Vera Vanderberg from Troy, who was friends with one of the victims, was brought to Albany where the suspect was transferred for identification. She immediately stated 'that's not him.' The suspect was further questioned about the letter but stayed silent. He was then ordered released."

North Adams, Massachusetts

December 18th, 1911

"An arrest was made at the depot of the Boston and Maine Railway by Captain Peron and an officer of the North Adams police force of a man suspected in the killing of the Morner family in Defreestville, NY. An Italian found asleep at the Williamstown station said he walked from Mechanicville, NY and looked like he had been outside for days. He gave his name as Charles Alli and then Antonio Cerato. The man was later determined to be Beniameni Di Donato. He had made many conflicting statements, began to sob and acted hysterical when questioned. Milk dealer Horatio Mould who knew Donato, said the suspect was not him. Judge C.T. Phelps of the North Adams District Court ordered the man's discharge."

Many other suspects of Italian decent were detained, questioned then released. Geri Servo was arrested in Troy, New York. Pasquale Paris arrested in Rochester, New York. Vittorino Tatasciori arrested in Meriden, Connecticut and Bartholomew Salerno in Long Island City, New York.

Some arrests occurred as far away as Dickinson, North Dakota where a man who gave his name as Edward Donato was in custody but later released when a photograph sent to Rensselaer proved the man was not the Donato we had been looking for. Despite the gallant efforts of my colleagues, the case is only getting colder.

A few days later I called a press conference to update the community on our progress. Something came over me this day. The cool callus shell I wore as a lawman was melting and a mass of soul searching crept in. A switch flipped. The opposite switch that flipped in Donato. Mine was a song of enlightenment. Before becoming sheriff, I was a school teacher. It was my intellectual ability that got me this job and this case has left me feeling profoundly retrospective. I'm reminded how our time here is short and to love everything you have because you're not going to have it forever. Be funny, be kind, be weird. Say everything in your heart to everyone that matters. Right now you're in the middle of what is going to flash before your eyes in the end. Don't waste a minute of it. I began with the announcement of appointing a new undersheriff, Mr. Henry W. Snell followed by the sobering news that Donato is likely headed for Italy. "We will continue our search for the man but at this time the trail has gone cold." I kept to myself the frustration that Donato may not be brought to justice. After a barrage of overlapping and incoherent questions quieted down, an inquisitive silence came over the room which I broke with these words: "In the years of devoting myself to keeping peace, I have seen death, dismemberment, good, evil and the truth that lies in a man's heart. There is one conclusion I have drawn from this life spent serving the public. It lies plainly in the words of the Reverend John Bulnes:

'Be ready for sudden death, set
thy house in order, for you do
not know when he comes.'

You're alive, go do something.
I wish you all a good day."

Epilogue

After the murders, Edward Donato was never seen again. It is believed he traveled to Boston where he boarded a ship back to Italy. Jesse Morner took over the farm and died on the property in 1945. The killing of the Morner family remains the worst crime in the history of Rensselaer County. It is said the farmhouse is haunted by the Morner family to this day.

www.ingramcontent.com/pod-product-compliance
Lightning Source LLC
Chambersburg PA
CBHW021000160726

47994CB00006B/2322